Steven's big loss . . .

Steven was absolutely miserable as he walked home from school on Wednesday afternoon. All he could think about was the election he'd lost that day. It was totally unfair. Ben was still new to Sweet Valley and nowhere near as popular as Steven. How would he ever survive the humiliation of losing to that dweeb?

As he turned onto his street, he kicked a big rock into the gutter. That's just what I'd like to do to that loser Ben Oliver, *Steven thought.* He's lucky I didn't punch him in the stomach right in front of everyone. The next time I see his ugly face, he won't be so lucky.

Steven walked up the front steps of his house and swung open the door. He froze.

Standing in the front hallway of his house talking to his sister was Ben Oliver!

Bantam Books in the SWEET VALLEY TWINS AND FRIENDS series.
Ask your bookseller for the books you have missed.

Sweet Valley Twins and Friends Super Editions

Sweet Valley Twins and Friends Super Chiller Editions

Sweet Valley Twins and Friends Magna Editions

SWEET VALLEY TWINS AND FRIENDS

Steven's Enemy

◇

Written by
Jamie Suzanne

Created by
FRANCINE PASCAL

BANTAM BOOKS
NEW YORK · TORONTO · LONDON · SYDNEY · AUCKLAND

RL 4, 008-012

STEVEN'S ENEMY
A Bantam Book / September 1994

*Sweet Valley High® and Sweet Valley Twins and Friends® are
registered trademarks of Francine Pascal*

Conceived by Francine Pascal

*Produced by Daniel Weiss Associates, Inc.
33 West 17th Street
New York, NY 10011*

Cover art by James Mathewuse

ISBN: 0-553-48097-9

Published simultaneously in the United States and Canada

*Bantam Books are published by Bantam Books, a division of Bantam
Doubleday Dell Publishing Group, Inc. Its trademark, consisting of the
words "Bantam Books" and the portrayal of a rooster, is Registered in
U.S. Patent and Trademark Office and in other countries. Marca
Registrada. Bantam Books, 1540 Broadway, New York, New York 10036.*

PRINTED IN THE UNITED STATES OF AMERICA

OPM   0 9 8 7 6 5 4 3 2 1

To Bobby Dean Phillips

One

◇

"Oh, give me a break," Lila Fowler said as she bit into a french fry. "Veronica Brooks is wearing the exact same outfit you wore yesterday, Jessica."

"You mean my new purple leggings and sweater?" Jessica Wakefield asked as she whirled around to see for herself. "The nerve of that girl. It's pathetic the way she copies us."

It was Monday, and Jessica was sitting in the Sweet Valley Middle School cafeteria with her friends in the Unicorn Club. The Unicorns were a group of the prettiest and most popular girls at school. They had their own table in the lunchroom, which they called the Unicorner.

The Unicorns were the envy of everyone in Sweet Valley Middle School—or at least they thought so. Purple, the color of royalty, was the official club color, so they each tried to wear at least one purple accessory or one article of purple clothing every day. Their favorite activities were shopping at the Valley Mall and talking about boys, parties, and clothes.

Veronica Brooks was new to Sweet Valley. Her family had moved into the mansion next door to the Fowlers' just a few months before. She was tall and pretty and had silky dark shoulder-length hair. She was also scheming and devious, which was why Jessica couldn't stand her.

Not long ago, Veronica had gone to extremes to try to become a Unicorn. Many of the Unicorns' belongings began mysteriously disappearing, and when the belongings turned up in Jessica's locker, the Unicorns decided to kick her out of the club. In the meantime, Veronica was spending a lot of time with the Unicorns and was ready to take Jessica's place. Luckily, Jessica's identical twin sister, Elizabeth, discovered the real thief—Veronica! Her theft was all a part of a plan to frame Jessica, and get her kicked out of the Unicorn Club so Veronica could become a Unicorn herself.

Jessica had never been so grateful to her twin sister before. The Wakefield sisters were completely identical on the outside, with the same blue-green eyes, the same long, sun-streaked blond hair, and the same dimple in their left cheek. But the similarities ended there. Elizabeth thought that the Unicorns were snobby and boring. She was much happier hanging out with one of her close friends, reading a book, or working on the *Sixers*, the school newspaper that she had helped start. Jessica thought Elizabeth's friends and favorite activities were about as exciting as a math test. Still, even though the sisters were different, they were best friends, and they knew they could count on each other for anything.

"You'd think Veronica would have changed schools by now. I mean, it's disgusting what she did to Jessica and the rest of us," Lila said as she flipped her long straight brown hair over her shoulder. Lila was Jessica's best friend after Elizabeth, and she was one of the wealthiest girls in Sweet Valley.

"I kind of enjoy seeing her face every day, since it's so totally green with envy," Jessica said. "Hey, Janet, can I have a bite of your hamburger?"

"Huh? Oh, yeah," Janet muttered. Janet was staring off into space, barely listening to anything anyone else was saying. She was an eighth grader and the president of the Unicorns. Jessica, a sixth grader, thought she was the coolest, and so did the rest of the Unicorns.

"Earth to Janet," Lila teased as she waved her hand in front of Janet's face. "What planet are you on?"

"Wait, don't tell me," Jessica said as she put her

fingers on either side of her head and closed her eyes. "I think I'm getting something. Janet is thinking about something tall, male, and handsome."

Everyone giggled, including Janet, who seemed to have been snapped out of her trance. "Wow, I guess you really are psychic," Janet said. Jessica had once claimed she was psychic, and she had even appeared on television to demonstrate her abilities. "I was just thinking of somebody who fits that exact description."

"You don't usually space out over Denny at lunch," Mary said. Denny Jacobson was Janet's steady boyfriend.

"Who? Oh, yeah, Denny. I'm taking a break from *him*." Janet leaned forward, an urgent expression on her face. "I'm getting so sick of him. All he can think about is his new computer game. Two nights ago we were talking on the phone, and he wouldn't stop playing this stupid tank game. I was trying to tell him about the Boosters' new routine, and I kept hearing things explode in the background." She shook her head sadly. "I think I need someone more mature."

"How is Denny taking the news?" Jessica asked.

"He'll survive," Janet said dismissively. "He was playing the tank game when I told him, so I'm not sure he even heard me. Anyway, it's just a temporary separation until he gets bored with this game, which I hope is soon."

"So where's the new guy?" Ellen asked as she scanned the lunchroom.

Janet sighed wistfully. "He's not here."

"Does he go to another school?" Tamara asked.

"Yes," Janet said dreamily, "he does."

"So which one does he go to? How did you meet him?" Jessica pressed.

"His name is Doug and he goes to Sweet Valley High," Janet boasted triumphantly. "He's a friend of Joe's from the basketball team and he came over yesterday for dinner. He's one of the cutest guys I've ever seen." Joe was Janet's brother, and he and Jessica's brother, Steven, were best friends. They were both freshmen at Sweet Valley High and played on the junior varsity basketball team together.

"So did you let him know you have a crush on him?" Jessica asked, taking another bite of Janet's hamburger. She figured Janet wouldn't notice since she was so spaced-out.

"Are you kidding? An eighth-grade girl can't just start flirting with a high school guy," Janet said authoritatively. "And yes, you may have another bite of my hamburger."

"Is this Janet Howell, the president of the Unicorn Club, speaking?" Lila asked incredulously. "When did any Unicorn not go after what she wanted?"

"I guess that *is* the Unicorn fighting spirit . . ." Janet said, her eyes twinkling.

"I've got a great idea!" Jessica announced, breaking into an enormous grin. "Let's all go to the junior-varsity basketball practice tomorrow! Janet can check out her hunk and we'll tell her whether we give our approval."

Janet made a face as if she'd eaten something sour. "I don't know, Jessica. I don't want Doug to think I'm chasing after him."

"Well, first of all, you *are* chasing after him, but he doesn't have to know that," Jessica said. "Besides, it's totally normal for us to go watch them practice. After all, my brother and Janet's brother are on the team, so Doug will just think we're there to watch them."

"Just imagine how cool it would be if a Unicorn started dating a high school guy," Lila said excitedly. "It would be great for our reputation."

"Yeah, everyone would be even more jealous of us than they usually are," Jessica said, looking around the lunchroom. "And I know one person who would be the most jealous of all."

"Veronica Brooks!" the Unicorns all said in unison.

"But that's *my* position," Steven Wakefield pleaded on Monday afternoon. "I've been playing starting center all season."

"And you've been doing a fine job, but I want to give Ben Oliver a chance at it," Coach Sloane said, pacing up and down the sidelines of the Sweet Valley High basketball court. "Switching positions is good for each individual player and for the team as a whole. Besides, Steven, playing guard is just as important as playing center."

Yeah, right, Steven thought resentfully. *No way is playing guard anything like playing the starting center. Before, I was the star of the team.* How could a dork like Ben Oliver take his place? Steven felt his whole body shaking from head to toe. *Ben Oliver! The guy has loser written all over him!* Steven thought as he sat down on the bench.

Ben Oliver was a freshman in high school like Steven, but he was a year younger because he skipped seventh grade. And just because he'd skipped one measly grade, it seemed as though he thought he was superior to everyone else. Whenever their biology teacher called on Ben, he would always have to give some long, complicated answer. He was such a show-off! Plus, Ben was always acting like Mr. Nice Guy toward Steven. As far as Steven was concerned, there was nothing more infuriating than when a guy you hated acted really nice to you.

The only thing that made Steven feel any better was the fact that he and Ben were both running for freshman-class treasurer. After losing his position on the team, Steven was more fired up than ever to cream Ben in the election on Wednesday. He decided he would go home and write the greatest campaign speech in all of Sweet Valley High history that evening. *Watch out, Ben Oliver. You're about to enter a contest you'll wish you'd never started! Let's see you act like Mr. Nice Guy when I'm through with you!*

"Keep it down in there or I'll set off a stink bomb in your room!" Steven yelled, pounding his bedroom wall with his fist.

It was Monday evening before dinner and Steven was sitting at his desk working on his campaign speech—or trying to. He was having a hard time concentrating on all of his outstanding qualifications because of the racket coming from the next room—Jessica's room.

Why did she pick the day he wrote the greatest speech in his political career to have one of her ridiculous Unicorn meetings? Steven thought the Unicorns were unbelievably annoying. They yacked for hours and hours about boys and clothes and hair products. And when they weren't gossiping, they were giggling, which was even worse. *How can they be so irritating when an important campaign speech is being written in the next room?* Steven thought as he sat back down at his desk.

"'Ladies and gentlemen, members of the faculty, and my fellow students,'" Steven read out loud to himself. "'It is with great pleasure that I stand here before you today to discuss some of the issues facing our school—'"

Steven stopped reading. Something seemed wrong. There was total silence. *Since when do those girls shut up that easily? I must have really scared them,* he thought with satisfaction.

"Eh-hem," he began again. "'I stand here before you today to discuss—'"

This time he heard something on the other side of his door. The noise had the distinct and irritating sound of a girl's giggle. He crossed his room and flung open the door.

"Get away from my room!" Steven yelled at the cluster of startled Unicorns in the hallway.

Jessica and her friends quickly ran down the hall, barely containing their giggles. Steven slammed his door and stormed back to his desk. The only thing worse than listening to girls giggle while he tried to write a campaign speech was listening to girls giggle *at* his campaign speech. As if Ben Oliver's stealing his position on the basketball team weren't enough! Now his stupid sister had to mess with him, too.

"Mom and Dad, I'd like to propose that Jessica not be allowed to have her stupid Unicorn meetings here anymore," Steven said at dinner as he poured almost an entire bottle of ketchup onto his meat loaf. "I was trying to write my campaign speech today and I couldn't get anything done."

Elizabeth was about to lose her appetite from looking at Steven's plate. *If he's going to make such a mess, he could at least eat the meat loaf. Why's he just letting it sit there in a mound of ketchup?*

"That's such a lie," Jessica said, grabbing the ketchup from Steven. "The Unicorns were having a perfectly innocent meeting. It's not *our* fault that Steven can't get his work done."

"Sorry, Jess, but I think Steven has a point," Elizabeth said as she fidgeted with the barrette in her hair. "There *was* a lot of noise coming from your room. I couldn't really concentrate on my science paper, either."

"I can't believe you're taking his side!" Jessica exclaimed, banging down her fork. "I thought sisters were supposed to stick together, stay united against the enemy brother!"

Mr. and Mrs. Wakefield looked first at each other and then at Jessica. "Honey," Mrs. Wakefield began sweetly, "I think you really have to listen to what your brother and sister are saying. There are five people living in this house, and we all have to make accommodations for one another."

"Yeah, Mom's right," Steven said hotly. "I say

that from here on out, Jessica and her stupid, gossiping, loser friends are banned from ever meeting in this house again."

"Steven—" Mr. Wakefield began.

"You can't do that!" Jessica shrieked. "And you can't let him talk that way about me and my friends!"

"Calm down," Mr. Wakefield said to Jessica. "We're not going to ban your meetings. We're simply asking that you make an effort to keep the noise down in the future. And Steven, I want you to apologize to Jessica."

"Sorry," Steven muttered almost inaudibly. He slumped in his seat and kept his head down for most of the meal. When Mrs. Wakefield served a blueberry pie for dessert, Elizabeth noticed that Steven didn't even take a bite of his. *Something is definitely bugging him*, Elizabeth thought. *Usually he's a human garbage disposal.*

"Hey, Steven," Elizabeth said, putting down her fork. "What's wrong? You're not eating any pie."

"That's certainly not like you, Steven," Mrs. Wakefield said with a concerned expression. "Aren't you feeling well?"

"Actually," Steven said, staring down at his untouched plate, "I do have some bad news."

"What is it?" Mr. Wakefield asked.

"Don't tell me—you got a new pimple today," Jessica guessed, spearing a stray blueberry with her fork.

"Ha ha ha," Steven said, giving Jessica a threatening look.

"Don't pay any attention to Jessica," Mrs. Wakefield said. "Tell us what happened."

"It's pretty humiliating. The dweebiest show-off in my class just took my position as starting center," Steven said, crumpling his napkin into a ball.

"That's awful," Elizabeth said sympathetically. She knew basketball was one of the most important things in Steven's life. *He really does look upset,* she thought.

"Now I'm stuck playing guard," Steven said.

"Guards are just as important as centers," Mr. Wakefield said in a comfortable tone. "But I know you're disappointed."

"Disappointed?" Steven repeated incredulously. "I'm not just disappointed. I'm on the warpath. Ben's running against me for class treasurer, and I'm going to win by such a landslide he'll be sorry he ever tried to compete with me!"

Elizabeth watched as Steven plunged his fork into his pie and ate almost half the piece in one bite. *Now* that's *more like the Steven I know,* she thought.

Two

◇

"There, that should get everyone's attention. By to-morrow Ben Oliver will be history," Steven said to his girlfriend and campaign manager, Cathy Connors. It was Tuesday morning, and he had just taped a campaign poster to the wall in the main Sweet Valley High hallway. The poster said, "BE A WINNER WITH WAKEFIELD . . . OR A LOSER WITH OLIVER!"

"Don't you think that's a little mean?" Cathy asked as she stood back and studied the poster. "I mean, Ben's not really such a bad guy."

"Are you kidding me?" Steven asked as he turned to Cathy in disbelief. "He's an ugly, wimpy, conniving punk."

"Oh, come on, Steven. He's not ugly at all," Cathy argued. "In fact, I think he's really pretty cute."

Pretty cute! How dare she think he's pretty cute!
Steven thought angrily. "Maybe you need
glasses," he told her hotly as he combed his fingers through his dark hair. "Since you obviously
can't see him too clearly, I'll tell you what he is.
He's a shrimpy kid who thinks he's the greatest
thing to hit Sweet Valley High, and if *you* think
he's so great maybe you should be *his* campaign
manager instead of mine!"

"Calm down," Cathy said, trying not to giggle.
"All I said was that I think he's cute. I think
you're much cuter, and I don't want to be his
campaign manager. I'm your campaign manager,
and I'm going to keep being your campaign manager until the election's over and you're the next
class treasurer."

"Why are you laughing, then?" Steven was
still irritated but not quite as angry anymore.
"What's so funny?"

"You're so funny," Cathy said, kissing him on
the cheek.

"And why is that?" Steven asked.

"Because you're jealous," Cathy said. "I like
seeing you jealous."

"I'm not jealous," Steven said defensively.
"And I would never be jealous of someone as
dorky as Ben Oliver."

"Yes you are," Cathy teased as they walked
down the hallway.

"No I'm not," Steven retorted.

"Yes you are," Cathy repeated.

"Can I have a bite of your sloppy joe?" Elizabeth asked Amy Sutton on Tuesday in the middle school lunchroom. Amy was Elizabeth's best friend after Jessica, and the two girls spent a lot of time together working on *The Sweet Valley Sixers*.

"Sure, you can have the whole thing," Amy said quietly as she looked down at her plate. "I'm not very hungry."

"But you've barely touched it," Elizabeth said. "Are you feeling OK?"

"No, I'm just—" Amy broke off.

"What is it?" Elizabeth asked with concern. "Is something bothering you?"

Amy let out a heavy sigh and looked around to make sure nobody was listening to their conversation. "Do you promise not to repeat what I'm going to tell you?" Amy asked in an urgent whisper.

"Of course I promise," Elizabeth said as she leaned across the table to hear her friend better. "You don't even have to ask me that. You know anything you tell me is safe with me."

"It's about my parents," Amy said sadly.

"What's wrong?" Elizabeth asked in alarm.

"I'm not exactly sure what it is, to tell you the truth."

"Did you get in trouble for something?" Elizabeth asked. It was unlike Amy to be so vague about things. She was usually straight and to the point—just like Elizabeth.

"No, *I'm* not in trouble," Amy said, "but *they* might be. Lately, they've been acting really weird. Every time I walk into a room, they suddenly shut right up. They just stare at me, or at the floor. It's as if I'm interrupting some kind of terrible secret conversation."

"What kind of conversation? About what?" Elizabeth pressed.

"I don't know," Amy said. "They just seem really tense all the time. At dinner or breakfast they barely speak to each other. They usually communicate through me. Like, last night my mother said to me, 'Amy, tell your father that his dry cleaning is hanging in his closet,' even though my father was sitting right there at the table."

"Oh, Amy," Elizabeth said sympathetically. "That sounds awful for you."

"I'm so uncomfortable all the time that I can barely eat a whole meal."

"You do look like you've lost some weight," Elizabeth said, looking at her friend with concern. "You have to start eating, Amy. I command you to eat that whole sloppy joe." Elizabeth held the sandwich up to her friend.

Amy took a reluctant bite and put the sloppy

joe back down on her plate. "I'm just afraid that something horrible is going to happen," she said.

"Like what?" Elizabeth asked gently.

"Like my parents might get a divorce," Amy said, her eyes filling with tears.

Elizabeth reached across the table and held Amy's hand. "Don't assume the worst, Amy. Maybe you're just misunderstanding what's going on with them." *Divorce*—the word played over in Elizabeth's head. It was such an ugly word, and Elizabeth hoped that Amy was wrong. She *had* to be wrong. Reading so many mysteries had taught Elizabeth to be careful about making assumptions or jumping to conclusions. And Elizabeth even remembered one book by Amanda Howard, her favorite mystery writer, where a husband and wife were pretending their marriage was in trouble as part of a complicated plan to catch a thief. *The Suttons don't really seem like the thief-catching type, but you never know,* Elizabeth thought. *There has to be some good explanation for what's going on.*

Amy sighed. "I hope you're right."

"There really could be a million reasons why they're acting this way," Elizabeth said encouragingly. "And you and I are going to figure out what's going on and put an end to your worries once and for all!"

*   *   *

"And so I leave it to you, the members of the freshman class, to decide for yourselves who should be your next class treasurer," Steven said, his voice echoing around the school auditorium. He was trying to sound calm and in control. "The thing you want to ask yourselves when you cast your ballot tomorrow morning is, 'Who can I trust?' Remember, you have to trust the class treasurer with your money. The money we've all worked so hard to raise over the year. Do you want to put that trust in someone you barely know? Someone who hasn't been around all that long? I think not. Give your vote to the person most of you have known since you were in elementary school. That someone is me."

The auditorium filled with cheers and applause as Steven walked down the stairs from the stage. He was glad he'd given his speech after Ben. He thought it was best to be the last candidate to speak so the voters would remember him.

Steven scanned the room for Cathy and spotted her standing in the corner talking to Howie Farber. He walked up to her, looking forward to her great big smile and an even bigger hug.

"Hi, Steven," Cathy said unenthusiastically when he'd made his way over to her.

"So how'd I do?" Steven asked. He was beaming. He knew he'd knocked the socks off of Ben's speech.

"Fine. You did fine," she said blandly.

"Could you believe how boring Ben's speech was?" Steven asked, putting his hand over his mouth and pretending to yawn. "It looked like the entire front row was about to go to sleep."

"I don't know," Cathy said. "I didn't think it was *that* boring."

"Are you joking?" Steven asked as he straightened his tie. He'd worn a suit for the occasion, thinking it made him seem like a professional politician. "What does the economic state of America have to do with being the freshman-class treasurer of Sweet Valley High?"

"I think he was just trying to compare the economic hard times of the country with the hard times of the class budget or something," Cathy said.

"Yeah, he *tried*, all right, but come *on*. I mean, did he have to go on and on forever about it?" Steven said, exasperated. *Why does she keep defending him?* he wondered.

"Oh, well, whatever," Cathy said. "You were just fine today. I gotta go meet up with Howie. I'll see you later."

Steven watched as Cathy ran out of the auditorium. *She's in a weird mood*, he thought, but only for a second. *By this time tomorrow, Cathy will be psyched to be the girlfriend of the freshman class treasurer.* He left the auditorium with the stride of someone who was on the brink of a big win.

"Nice shot," Joe Howell said as Steven ran past him on the basketball court. It was Tuesday afternoon, and Steven had just sunk his fourth basket.

"Thanks," Steven said, dusting off his hands. "That ought to show the coach that I deserve my position back." Steven was having a good scrimmage at practice. He was running faster and shooting better than usual. *After today, Ben Oliver will be running out of this gym and back to Sweet Valley Middle School where he belongs*, Steven thought, imagining the expression on Ben's face when the coach told him that he wouldn't be playing starting center anymore.

"Ouch," Steven yelled as the basketball hit him on the head, interrupting his thoughts. Steven whirled around and saw Ben Oliver walking across the court toward him.

"Whoa, I'm really sorry," Ben said as he got closer to Steven. "I thought you saw me passing it to you."

"Quit dreaming, Wakefield," the coach shouted from the sidelines.

Dreaming? That no-good, rotten, sneaky Ben Oliver! He planned that! Steven thought as he glared into the eyes of his enemy. *Cut the phony innocent act, Oliver!* Steven turned on his heel and had begun to storm down the court when he heard a chorus of giggles. He looked over at the bleachers and saw Jessica and her Unicorn friends. They were all looking right at Steven and laughing.

Great, he thought, his heart sinking. *All I need is those silly girls laughing at me. I'm really going to get you for this, Oliver!*

"I think Doug just smiled at me," Janet cooed. "Did you guys just see that?"

"I think he was smiling because he scored a point," Lila said, rolling her eyes.

"No, I'm sure he was smiling at me," Janet insisted. "I think he's about the cutest guy I've ever seen. Don't you think so, Jessica?"

"He's gorgeous," Jessica said dreamily. "That thick dark-blond hair and those blue eyes are to die for!"

"Huh? Doug has *red* hair," Janet said, following Jessica's eyes across the court. "You've got the wrong guy, Jessica. You're looking at someone else. Doug is sitting on the bench, see?"

"I'm in love," Jessica gushed as she stared unblinkingly at the dark-blond, blue-eyed player.

"That guy you're looking at just smiled at you, Jessica!" Mandy Miller shrieked.

"I know!" Jessica was practically swooning.

"He's been smiling at me ever since we sat down here. I wonder who he is? He must be a new student or something. I've never noticed him at Steven's games before."

"Excuse me, but no one's noticing that Doug has been smiling at me the whole time, too," Janet pouted.

"Give it up, Janet," Lila teased. "He was probably just looking over here because you keep making goo-goo eyes at him. He probably thinks you have something in your eye."

"I can't believe how obnoxious you are, Lila. You're obviously blind," Janet said in a huff.

Normally, Jessica enjoyed listening to Janet and Lila squabbling, but now they and the other Unicorns seemed miles away. She had one thought on her mind—the adorable new player on the team. *I never realized how interesting basketball is*, she thought. *I'll have to start coming to more games and find out who that boy is!*

Three

◇

"OK, here's your chance, Janet," Tamara Chase said, poking Janet in the ribs as Doug walked out of the locker room. "Go up to him and say something."

The girls were waiting outside the locker room after practice on Tuesday, and Jessica's stomach was doing flip-flops. *Please let him come out and talk to me*, Jessica pleaded silently. She tossed her hair and let it fall around her shoulders.

"It's now or never," Mary Wallace urged Janet.

"What will I say?" Janet asked nervously.

"Tell him you got something in your eye and could he help you get it out," Lila joked.

"Very funny," Janet said.

"Just go," Ellen Riteman said, practically jumping up and down with excitement. "We'll be here for moral support. If he asks you out, give us the thumbs-up sign."

"OK, OK," Janet whispered giddily. "Wish me luck!" She walked casually toward the water fountain where Doug was getting a drink.

"Good luck," they said in unison, giggling.

The girls watched Janet's every move as she laughed and smiled with Doug. Finally, Janet looked at the Unicorns and gave them a quick thumbs-up, and the Unicorns gave one another silent high fives.

"Quick, somebody give me some lip gloss," Jessica commanded as the door to the locker room opened. Jessica took a deep breath as the gorgeous basketball player she'd spotted walked toward them. "Maybe Janet's good luck will rub off on me."

"Hey, did you all enjoy practice?" Jessica's crush asked the group.

"We loved it," Jessica said enthusiastically. "You were especially great."

"Aren't you Wakefield's sister?" he asked.

"That's right," Jessica said, beaming at him. "How did you know?"

"I asked one of the guys on the team," he said. "Are you a freshman?"

He asked who I was! He really was looking at me! And he thinks I'm in high school! Jessica thought excitedly.

"Yes, my friends and I are all freshmen," Jessica told him eagerly.

"No, we're not," Lila chimed in. "We're still in middle school. In fact, Jessica's in the sixth grade."

Jessica wished there were some subtle way she could kick Lila in the shin. "What I *meant* to say was that my brother Steven's a freshman," Jessica said, forcing a giggle.

"Funny, I thought you were in high school. You girls definitely look like you could be," the guy said, looking right at Jessica.

"Thanks, I *have* always been told that I look old for my age," Jessica said, brushing her hair back from her face with her hand.

"Well, I guess I should get going. Oh, by the way, what's your name?" he asked Jessica.

"Jessica. What's yours?" she asked breathlessly.

"Ben Oliver," he said, shaking Jessica's hand.

Ben Oliver. A perfect name for a perfect guy, Jessica thought as she floated out of the gym.

"Hey, Jess, did you do the take-home math quiz yet?" Elizabeth asked, walking into the family room. It was Tuesday night after dinner and Steven and Jessica were watching a basketball game on television.

"I'll do it tomorrow during homeroom," Jessica said, her eyes glued to the TV screen. "Wow! That was a great shot!"

"Yeah, Charles Hinley is probably going to win Rookie of the Year," Steven said.

"I think he's even better than George Farlin," Jessica said authoritatively.

Elizabeth sat on the couch next to Jessica and looked at her in disbelief. "Excuse me, but am I in the right house? Is that my sister, Jessica Wakefield, or did some phantom basketball fan just sneak into her body during dinner?"

"No, it's me," Jessica answered distractedly.

"Well, the Jessica I know never watched a basketball game and actually paid attention to it," Elizabeth said.

"Really, Elizabeth, what do you think we Boosters are doing at basketball games and practices?" Jessica asked. Jessica was a member of the Boosters, the baton and cheering squad for Sweet Valley Middle School.

"I never noticed you ever watching the games," Elizabeth said. "You guys mostly smile at the crowd and whisper to one another."

"Well, maybe I didn't pay all that much attention in the past," Jessica said defensively. "But I just realized what a fascinating game it is."

"You *just* realized it? Why do I get the feeling that this sudden realization has to do with a certain basketball *player*?" Elizabeth asked. "Who is he?"

"Who's who?" Jessica asked innocently.

"Who's suddenly turned you into a basketball expert?" Elizabeth asked knowingly.

"OK I admit it. He's the cutest, most adorable guy I've ever seen in my life," Jessica gushed. "He has beautiful, dark-blond hair and the cutest smile in the world."

"Oh, please, you're making me nauseous," Steven said, holding his stomach.

"Sorry, Steven, but nothing you say can bother me, because I'm in love!" Jessica said proudly.

"But what about Aaron?" Elizabeth asked. "I thought *he* was the cutest, most adorable guy you'd ever seen in your life." Aaron Dallas was Jessica's on-and-off boyfriend.

"Aaron's great," Jessica said, "but he's only in the sixth grade."

"The last I heard you were only in the sixth grade yourself," Steven said, rolling his eyes.

"Everyone knows that girls mature faster than boys," Jessica said matter-of-factly. "I need someone who's more up to my speed."

"Jessica! Telephone for you!" Mrs. Wakefield yelled from the kitchen.

Jessica leapt up from the floor. "Cross your fingers that it's him!" she said to Elizabeth as she ran out of the room. "Steven, tell me what I miss while I'm gone."

Please be him. Please be him. Please be him, Jessica repeated over and over again to herself as she rushed across the kitchen. Jessica grabbed the phone from her mother. "Hello?" she said breathlessly into the receiver.

"Hi, Jessica? It's Ben Oliver. I met you today after basketball practice."

It's him! Jessica thought euphorically. *A high school guy is calling me on the phone! All the Unicorns are going to flip when I tell them!* "Hi, Ben," Jessica said, trying to sound calm and grown up. "Can you hold on a minute?" Jessica put her hand over the receiver and turned to her mother, who was finishing up the dinner dishes.

"Mom," she whispered, "would you mind giving me a little privacy for a minute?"

Mrs. Wakefield smiled and shook her head, then walked out of the kitchen.

"So hi again," Jessica said, giggling slightly. "I was just watching the basketball game on TV. Were you?"

"No, I was working on my acceptance speech for the class treasurer in case I get elected tomorrow," Ben said. "Are you a basketball fan?"

"Am I a fan? I love basketball!" Jessica gushed. "I never miss a game."

"That's pretty cool," Ben said.

As happy as she was to be talking to Ben, Jessica was also dying to get off the phone so she could call her friends and tell them he'd called. She could just imagine their reactions. They would be totally impressed and totally jealous at the same time. Lila would probably try to sound bored, but really she'd be seething with envy.

Ben kept going on and on about the campaign. Jessica was beginning to think she'd never get to call her friends. "And I really want to win. I think I would be perfect for the job, but I don't know—the competition is pretty tough."

"Uh-huh," Jessica muttered. *Who will I call first, Janet or Lila? Lila will probably be so mad and jealous that she'll hang up right away and call all the other Unicorns,* Jessica thought excitedly.

"So would you like to go out sometime?" Ben asked.

"Hmm?" Jessica said distractedly.

"I said, would you like to go out sometime?"

Jessica almost screamed with happiness. *He just asked me to go out! A high school guy just asked me out!* It was too good to be true. She took a deep breath, hoping she wouldn't sound overeager. "Sure," she said sweetly but casually.

"How about going to Casey's tomorrow for a sundae?" he asked.

"That sounds great," Jessica said. *Tomorrow afternoon! That gives me less than twenty-four hours to decide what to wear!*

"Good. So I'll come by your house after school," Ben said. "I asked one of the guys on the team where you live. I did my homework." Ben giggled. *A sort of goofy giggle*, Jessica thought. Obviously, he thought he'd made a funny joke.

Jessica said good-bye, hung up the phone, and picked it up again to call Lila. *A date with a high school guy! I'll be the envy of the whole school!*

"Ladies and gentlemen, members of the faculty, and my fellow students. It is with great pleasure and modesty that I accept your unanimous decision that I serve you as treasurer of our fine freshman class."

The crowd was cheering wildly as Steven stood on the stage behind the podium. Girls were throwing roses at Steven's feet and people were waving life-size posters of Steven in the air.

Cathy ran up to Steven and threw her arms around him. "You're the greatest!" she gushed as she smothered him in kisses. "You're the smartest, most handsome, and best-basketball-playing freshman-class treasurer in the entire state of California!"

Steven looked over and saw Ben Oliver crouched down in the corner of the auditorium. Tears were streaming down his face, and people were pointing and laughing at him.

"You'll never play basketball again," their coach was yelling to Ben. "In fact, you are to report immediately back to seventh grade where you belong. You should never have been allowed in this school in the first place."

The school band started playing "For He's a Jolly

*Good Fellow" and a group of guys picked Steven up
and carried him around the auditorium on their shoulders. . . .*

The alarm clock started buzzing right in
Steven's ear and he sat straight up in bed. It took
him a minute to realize that he'd only been
dreaming. It had seemed so real that he'd woken
up feeling overjoyed and triumphant.

*Maybe that was a dream, but today it's going to be-
come reality!* he thought confidently.

"Hairnet will have a total conniption fit!" Ken
Matthews was saying to Todd Wilkins. It was
Wednesday morning and they were standing at
the water fountain in the middle school hallway.
"I can't wait to see the look on her face when—"

"When what?" Elizabeth asked as she snuck
up on them. Todd was Elizabeth's sort-of boyfriend and she could tell from the look on his face
that they had some good gossip about Mrs.
Arnette, the social studies teacher the students
referred to as "Hairnet." Elizabeth usually didn't
care about gossip, but as the editor of the *Sixers*,
she thought she should know what was going
on, especially when it concerned teachers.

"Hi, Elizabeth," Todd said, swinging around
and flashing a smile. Elizabeth thought he was
the cutest guy in the school, with his wavy dark
hair and brown eyes.

"Don't 'hi' me," she teased. "Tell me why Mrs. Arnette is going to have a conniption."

"What's she talking about?" Ken asked Todd, pretending to look confused.

"Beats me," Todd said.

"Come on," Elizabeth pressed. "What's going on?"

"Hi, Todd!"

Elizabeth looked over her shoulder and saw Veronica Brooks walking down the hall toward them, waving at Todd.

Don't let her get to you, Elizabeth told herself. Earlier that semester, Veronica had tried to steal Todd away from her. And Veronica was always flirting with Todd in front of Elizabeth, just to make her mad. Normally, Elizabeth tried to see the best in people, but Veronica Brooks was one of the few people that Elizabeth couldn't stand.

"Did I ever tell you how much I like that T-shirt?" Todd asked Elizabeth.

"Did I ever tell you how much I like it when you tell me newsworthy information?" Elizabeth asked.

"We really can't get anything past you, can we?" Ken asked. "I guess that's why you're such an ace reporter."

"Spare me the compliments, guys," Elizabeth said, putting her hands on her hips.

"OK, you win," Todd said.

"You're not going to tell her, are you?" Ken asked. "She'll just print it in the *Sixers* and it will ruin the surprise."

"I promise not to put it in the *Sixers*," Elizabeth said, crossing her fingers. She didn't like to lie, but if it was the only way of getting a good story, she was willing to bend her rule a little.

"Well, I won't tell you everything, but I'll give you a hint," Todd said, leaning toward her and lowering his voice. "Some guys in the seventh grade are planning a little treat for Hairnet's class next Wednesday."

"What kind of treat?" Elizabeth asked. "You have to give me a bigger hint than that."

"A four-legged treat," Todd said, winking at Ken.

"A four-legged treat?" Elizabeth said thoughtfully. "Does it bark or squeak, by any chance?"

"Nope," Todd said. "And there's the bell. Time for class."

Elizabeth watched them hurry down the hall. She was determined to find out what the surprise was going to be before Wednesday. She desperately needed a juicy story for the next issue of the *Sixers*. And once she put her mind to a story, she wouldn't let it go until she'd figured it out.

Four

◇

"And the next president of the freshman class is . . . Shauna Colwin!" Mr. Cooper announced in home room on Wednesday morning.

Everyone was cheering and applauding—everyone except Steven. He was sitting next to Cathy, crossing his fingers. *And the next treasurer of the freshman class is Steven Wakefield,* he chanted over and over in his head. He looked over at Ben, who was smiling calmly. *I wouldn't be so calm if I were you, Ben Oliver,* he thought, stifling a snicker.

"And the next vice-president of the freshman class is Yvonne Jones," Mr. Cooper announced. Again the room was full of cheers and applause.

"This is it," Steven whispered nervously to Cathy. "This is the moment I've been waiting for. I'm going to win this hands down."

Cathy smiled weakly at Steven. "I hope you're right."

There she goes, acting weird again, Steven thought. *Maybe she's just nervous for me.*

"If I can have everyone's undivided attention," Mr. Cooper started. "Please calm down."

Steven's stomach was full of butterflies. *Just say it! "And the winner is Steven Wakefield!"*

"The votes for class treasurer are too close to call," Mr. Cooper said. "We're going to have another vote this afternoon and the results will be announced at three o'clock."

"Did he say what I think he said?" Steven asked Cathy.

"I'm afraid so," Cathy said. "You'll just have to wait a few more hours."

"But I can't wait another minute!" Steven said. "There must be some mistake. I'm going to talk to Cooper. I'm sure I beat that punky Oliver by a landslide."

"I wouldn't if I were you," Cathy cautioned. "You might just aggravate him. Just try to put it out of your mind for the day."

"Put it out of my mind for the day?" Steven asked in disbelief. "How am I supposed to concentrate on anything besides beating Oliver? I wish I could just fall asleep and wake up at three."

"You know, maybe it wouldn't be the worst

thing in the world if you lost the election," Cathy said timidly. "Think about all the extra time you'll have if you don't win. It's a huge responsibility to be class treasurer."

Steven stared at Cathy in shock. "Did you hit your head or something?"

"No, of course not," Cathy said. "Why?"

"Well, you're acting totally delirious," Steven said. "You know how much this election means to me. I can't believe that you would even suggest that I might be happier losing than winning."

"All I'm saying is maybe you should prepare yourself for the possibility that you could lose," Cathy said, standing up. "I mean, if the results from the first vote were that close, it could go either way."

"I'm going to pretend we never had this conversation," Steven said curtly as he stood up and threw his backpack over his shoulder.

"I've got a great story for the *Sixers*," Elizabeth said to Amy. It was Wednesday and Amy was standing at her locker in the school hallway before lunch. "There's a rumor going around that a group of guys are planning some big prank during Mrs. Arnette's class next week. Maybe we can find out what it is before it happens."

"Yeah, that sounds good," Amy said distractedly.

"I want us to do some snooping around to-morrow after school and see what we can come up with," Elizabeth said excitedly. "All they would tell me was that it was something that had four legs."

"Four legs," Amy repeated, staring off into space.

"They did mention that the guys involved were in the seventh grade," Elizabeth said, her eyes narrowing. "I bet you anything Bruce Patman is involved." Bruce Patman was the wealthiest guy at Sweet Valley Middle School, and most of the girls thought that he was the handsomest. Jessica and Elizabeth thought he was conceited and obnoxious, although Jessica did flirt with him occasionally.

"I'm sure you're right," Amy almost whispered. She looked down at the floor, then back up at Elizabeth. She had that faraway look she'd had the day before.

"Amy, what's wrong?" Elizabeth asked. "Is it your parents?"

Amy nodded. "Yes," she said sadly. "Last night I was walking down the hall and I heard my mom crying in the bedroom with the door shut."

"Was your father there?" Elizabeth asked.

"No. My mother said he had to work late at the office. The two of us ate dinner together in silence. Every time I tried to bring up something to say, she just uttered 'yes' or 'no.' When I told her that I got an A on that paper I did last week for social studies class, all she said was, 'Oh.' Usually, she's really excited when I tell her about my grades. Finally, I stopped trying to make conversation, because it was obvious that she didn't want to talk."

"Oh, Amy, I know that must feel terrible," Elizabeth said compassionately. "I hate for you to have to go through this kind of thing." Elizabeth couldn't imagine eating dinner at her house in silence. There was always so much talking and joking going on—not to mention squabbling—at the dinner table. She'd seen her mother cry at sad movies, but that was all. *How awful to see your mom cry when you couldn't talk to her about what made her sad,* Elizabeth thought.

"I just don't know what to do," Amy went on sadly. "I feel so helpless, because I'm afraid to ask her what's going on. I'm not sure I want to know the truth."

"I have an idea," Elizabeth said. "We need to get to the bottom of this. How about if I spend the night at your house on Friday and we'll see what we can come up with? My detective instincts tell me that we shouldn't assume it's a problem with their marriage. We'll find out what's really going on."

Amy smiled a little. "My parents are going out on Friday night, so your plan is perfect. What would I do without you, Detective Wakefield?"

"You'll never have to know," Elizabeth said. *I just hope we don't find something terrible*, she thought as they walked down the hall to their social studies class.

"Here comes Mr. Cooper," Cathy whispered to Steven. It was Wednesday afternoon, and the sound of laughter and gossip filled the auditorium. "Don't you think you'd have a better view if you took your face out of your hands?"

Steven couldn't look at anyone until he'd heard the announcement. "I will when he says that I'm the next class treasurer," Steven said between his fingers.

"Please quiet down, everyone," Mr. Cooper said into the microphone. "After taking a second vote I am pleased to announce that the next treasurer of the freshman class will be . . ."

Steven Wakefield. Steven Wakefield, Steven was chanting in his head.

". . . Ben Oliver!"

Steven jerked his hands away from his face and looked up at the stage. The clapping and cheering all around him seemed far away as Mr. Cooper's fatal words repeated themselves over and over in his head. *But I'm supposed to be class treasurer!* he thought miserably. *This has to be a mistake! They must have counted wrong!*

Steven felt as though he was about to be sick. Now Ben had beaten him out of his position on the basketball team *and* in the election. He hated Ben Oliver more than he'd ever hated anyone.

"I'm really sorry," Cathy said, putting her hand gently on Steven's shoulder. "You should have won. But look at the bright side—at least you won't have all the headaches that go along with being the treasurer."

"But I *want* all the headaches of being class treasurer," Steven muttered, standing up weakly. He felt someone tapping on his shoulder. He turned around and saw the face of his enemy staring back at him.

The sight of Ben's face made Steven shake all over with anger. *"What?"* Steven asked fiercely.

Ben extended his hand, but Steven just looked at it with disgust. "I just wanted to say that I hope there aren't any hard feelings. You ran a great campaign," Ben said sheepishly.

Steven stared at Ben for a moment, then turned away. "Come on, Cathy, let's get out of here," Steven said through clenched teeth. *I can't believe that two-faced weasel thinks I'd fall for his Mr. Nice Guy act after he tried to ruin my life,* Steven thought grimly as he headed for the door. *If Cathy weren't here, I'd stick around and punch his lights out.* "I'm starting to smell a rat," he added loudly enough for Ben to hear.

"What time is Ben picking you up?" Ellen asked Jessica as she twirled a baton in the air. It was Wednesday afternoon and the Boosters were practicing in the school gymnasium.

"He said he'd come by around five o'clock," Jessica said as she broke into the splits. "Which means I have to leave soon to get ready. I have to wash and blow-dry my hair and I still haven't decided what I'm wearing."

"Geez, Jessica, you're only going to Casey's," Lila said, rolling her eyes. "It's not like you're going to a ball or anything."

You're just jealous and you know it, Lila Fowler, Jessica thought as she watched Lila do a cartwheel. *You'd go nuts if a high school guy offered you a stick of gum.* Even though Lila was Jessica's best friend after Elizabeth, the two girls were always competing with each other.

"Since he's in high school, I'm sure he's used to girls who are a little more sophisticated than middle schoolers," Jessica said, flipping her hair to her right shoulder. "I was actually thinking I'd wear my new purple silk blouse with jeans. You know the blouse I'm talking about, don't you, Lila?"

"Yes," Lila said through gritted teeth.

"The one they'd already sold out of by the time you went to the store to buy it," Jessica pressed.

"I said, I *know* which blouse you're talking about," Lila said, her face turning red. "You don't have to rub it in."

"I heard that Aaron's really bummed that you're going out with Ben," Tamara said. "In homeroom he was all slouched over."

Jessica felt a little pang of guilt at the mention of her sort-of boyfriend. But she had more important things to worry about right now. In just a few hours she would be going on a date with a high school guy! "I'm sure he'll get over it," Jessica said, trying to sound unconcerned.

Janet turned to Jessica. "I was thinking that since Doug and I might become an item, we could double-date with you and Ben if you guys start seeing each other."

"That would be fantastic!" Jessica gloated. "You and Doug, and me and Ben! Both of us together with our high school guys!" Jessica glanced at Lila, pleased to see that her face was turning even redder.

"Ben will probably introduce you to his friends and you'll start spending time with them," Mary said as she did a back bend. "I hope you won't forget about us."

"Oh, I won't," Jessica said calmly, but inside

she was practically exploding at the thought. *Imagine! I'll go shopping and to the movies and to the Dairi Burger with high school students! I'll be the coolest sixth grader around, no question.* Jessica bounded out of the gym full of excitement.

Steven was absolutely miserable as he walked home from school on Wednesday afternoon. All he could think about was the election he'd lost that day. It was totally unfair. Ben was still new to Sweet Valley and nowhere near as popular as Steven. How would he ever survive the humiliation of losing to that dweeb?

As he turned in to his street, he kicked a big rock into the gutter. *That's just what I'd like to do to that loser Ben Oliver,* Steven thought. *He's lucky I didn't punch him in the stomach right in front of everyone. The next time I see his ugly face, he won't be so lucky.*

Steven walked up the front steps of his house and swung open the door. He froze.

Standing in the front hallway of *his* house talking to *his* sister was Ben Oliver!

Five

◇

"What is *he* doing here?" Steven shouted at Jessica.

"Steven!" Jessica exclaimed. "What's the matter with you?"

"You have a lot of nerve coming here to gloat over the election and rub it in my face!" Steven shouted, looking Ben dead in the eye. Steven was so red with fury, it looked to Jessica as though he was about to hit her date.

"Steven!" Jessica cried again. What was going on? Why was her brother butting into her life like this? It was unbelievable, even for Steven. "Would you calm down? This is Ben Oliver. He's picking me up to go to Casey's. And anyway, it's none of your business."

"I know *exactly* who he is!" Steven was shaking from head to toe. Jessica had never seen her brother so mad. "If you think you're going out with that piece of garbage, you're wrong! No sister of mine is leaving the house with Ben Oliver in my lifetime!"

Jessica looked worriedly at Ben, whose face was turning paler by the second.

"Maybe I should just go," Ben muttered quietly to Jessica.

"No! We're leaving together. I'm sorry about Steven. He's obviously losing his mind," Jessica said, grabbing Ben's arm. Then she turned to face Steven. "You have no right to tell me what to do, Steven Wakefield."

"I forbid you to leave this house with him," Steven said, ignoring her protest. He stood right in front of the door with his arms folded over his chest.

"In case you didn't get it the first time, Steven, you can't forbid me to do anything," Jessica said.

Taking Ben by the hand, she pushed past Steven out the front door and slammed it behind her.

"I'm so sorry about my demented brother," Jessica said to Ben across the booth at Casey's. They were each eating large hot-fudge sundaes. Jessica was eating hers super slowly in order to calm herself down about Steven's insane outburst. That, and she didn't want to spill anything on her purple silk blouse. "I don't know what's up with him. I mean, he's pretty weird normally, but this goes beyond anything I've ever experienced."

"I know why he's mad at me," Ben said, smoothing back his dark-blond hair.

"You do?" Jessica asked.

"Yeah, well, I beat him in the election today for class treasurer," Ben explained. "And on Monday, the coach gave me his usual position on the basketball team. It's really a bummer. I didn't mean anything personally. Steven actually seems like an OK guy. I wish we could've been friends."

"Friends with Steven? Trust me, it's no great loss. Consider yourself lucky," Jessica said knowingly. *This is even more interesting than I thought it would be*, Jessica mused. *I'm not dating just any high school guy but* the *high school guy who beat Steven out of his position on the basketball team and in the school election.*

Just then Jessica noticed that the Unicorns were sitting at a booth in the front of the restaurant. *Perfect.* They obviously wanted to watch her on her date.

"So I figured out a really great thing to do for my science project," Ben said cheerfully.

"Uh-huh," Jessica muttered. *From where they're sitting, can they see the way he's smiling at me?* she wondered. She tried not to look over at the Unicorns' table. She stared meaningfully into Ben's eyes so that her friends would see how intense they were.

"I'm working out a master plan that would involve using solar energy to turn on a computer," Ben went on.

"Hmmmm." Jessica smiled and tried to look interested. Her eyes drifted to the front of the restaurant, where she saw Aaron sitting in a booth with his friends. He was making everyone laugh as usual. *Aaron never goes on and on about a science project*, Jessica thought. *He's always so funny and tells great stories*. But she commanded herself not to miss him. *What's a guy who can tell a few funny stories compared with a totally cute high school guy? And now that I'm going out with Ben, every girl in school will wish they were me!*

"Where are Mom and Dad?" Jessica asked Elizabeth on Thursday morning as she came into the Wakefields' sunny Spanish-tiled kitchen. Steven and Elizabeth were sitting at the kitchen table eating breakfast.

"They left for work early," Elizabeth said. She looked over at Steven, who was being unusally quiet. She noticed he was cutting his French toast into little star shapes. She giggled. "Steven, wake up. You're not in arts-and-crafts class."

Steven glanced up at Elizabeth. "Huh?"

Jessica poured herself a glass of orange juice and sat down at the table. "So Elizabeth, did I mention that at the end of our fantastic date yesterday, Ben asked me if I wanted to go bowling tomorrow night?" Jessica asked breathlessly, looking directly at Steven.

"Actually, you told me that three times already," Elizabeth said.

"I guess I'm just so excited about Ben," Jessica gushed. "He's such a great guy. He's a great basketball player, and he's obviously really popular, since he just won the election for class treasurer."

Steven pushed his plate of little French-toast stars away and stood up. "That's it!" he yelled. "You're not going out with Ben ever again and I don't want to hear his name spoken in this house!"

"Geez, Steven, what's the matter?" Elizabeth asked, shocked. "What do you have against this guy?"

"Why don't you ask your sister?" Steven said venomously.

Elizabeth turned to Jessica in bewilderment. "Well? Can *you* tell me what's going on?"

"Why don't you ask your brother?" Jessica said huffily.

Elizabeth turned back to Steven.

"Fine," Steven said. "Jessica's decided that of

all the guys in Sweet Valley, she's going to go out with the jerk who beat me out of class treasurer and stole my position on the basketball team!"

"My love life is none of your business, Steven. But if you had any clue, you'd see what a great couple *Ben Oliver* and I make!" Jessica yelled back. "And by the way, I think you're acting like a real baby about that election. Ben can't help it if he's more popular than you and a better basketball player."

Steven's face turned a shade of red Elizabeth had never seen on someone who wasn't badly sunburned. "Mark my words, Jessica. If you go through with this, you'll be sorry!" He turned around and stomped out of the kitchen.

"I better go . . . um, change my socks," Elizabeth said, quickly getting up before her twin could start complaining to her about Steven.

This is one mess I want to stay out of, she thought, running up the stairs. *It looks like World War III at the Wakefields', and I don't want to get caught in the line of fire!*

"Who wants to explain what the Emancipation Proclamation was?" Mrs. Arnette asked her social studies class on Thursday morning. "Jessica, what about you?"

Jessica was staring out the window, trying to decide what to wear on her upcoming date with Ben.

She wanted to look pretty, of course, but she also needed to dress appropriately for bowling. *Maybe I'll borrow something from Elizabeth*, she thought.

"Jessica," Mrs. Arnette said sternly.

"Me?" she asked, suddenly shaken out of her thoughts.

"I asked you to explain the Emancipation Proclamation. It was in your reading last night," Mrs. Arnette said.

Jessica bit her lip. *Why does she have to call on me today of all days?* she thought. She was so busy talking on the phone the night before, telling all her friends about her date at Casey's and her date on Friday night, that she didn't get around to doing the reading.

"Can't you stand up and pretend to be me?" Jessica whispered to Elizabeth, who was sitting next to her. She knew that Elizabeth would have done the reading.

"Sorry, Jess," Elizabeth whispered. "You'll have to get out of this one yourself."

"We're waiting, Jessica," Mrs. Arnette said.

"Well, the Emancipation Proclamation was . . . well, a proclamation about emancipation," Jessica answered finally.

"I know what it was," a voice from the back of the classroom chirped loudly.

Jessica turned around and saw that the voice belonged to none other than Veronica Brooks!

Jessica's blood boiled as her enemy stood up and gave some boring, sickeningly long answer.

"Thank you, Veronica, that was a very astute and thoughtful explanation," Mrs. Arnette said. Then Mrs. Arnette looked back at Jessica with disapproval.

Jessica glared at Veronica, who had a hideous, smug smile pasted on her face. *What a phony little goody-goody*, Jessica thought. *I would have thought she'd learned not to mess with Jessica Wakefield by now!*

Steven trudged out of school on Thursday afternoon still in a bad mood from breakfast that morning. He was supposed to meet Cathy on the front lawn, but when he spotted her under a tree he almost had a fit. Sitting right next to her on the grass was Ben Oliver! And to make matters worse, Joe Howell—Steven's best friend—was sitting with them, too!

What is this? Some kind of conspiracy? Steven thought gloomily. *First my sister, now my girlfriend and my best friend? It's like he's trying to take over my whole life!*

Steven marched in their direction. "Cathy! Let's go!" he shouted from a few yards away.

Cathy stood up and walked toward Steven. He took her arm and pulled her away from the lawn.

"What were you doing with *him*?" Steven asked angrily.

"With who? Joe or Ben?" Cathy asked, obviously confused by Steven's behavior.

"Who do you think? My enemy—Ben Oliver," Steven said. He felt totally betrayed by Cathy, and he couldn't help himself from being jealous. She *had* said that she thought he was cute.

"Steven, I really don't think you should treat him like your enemy," Cathy said. "He's actually a nice guy. I think you should give him a chance. If you got to know him better, I bet you'd really like him."

Like him? Like Ben Oliver? Is she joking? Steven was outraged. "I can't believe you and Joe are so fooled by that phony. You don't even see his flaws."

"What flaws?" Cathy asked.

"Well . . ." Steven was stumped. He *knew* what Ben's flaws were, but it was hard to *say* exactly what they were. "Well, he's two-faced for one thing. He acts like he's my buddy and at the same time he's ruining my life behind my back."

"It's really not his fault that he won the election," Cathy said gently. "It's not like he ran against you just to be mean."

"You and my sister should get together and start an 'I love Ben' club," Steven said sourly.

"Oh, come on, Steven, you're being silly,"

Cathy said. "I still don't understand exactly what you think is wrong with him."

"If you can't figure it out for yourself, then I'm not going to stand here and explain it to you," Steven said. "Let's go back to your house. I don't want to see or talk about that creep for the rest of my life."

"What happens if Bruce or Mr. and Mrs. Patman come home?" Amy asked Elizabeth as they walked around the Patmans' backyard. "We're trespassing on their property. They could have us arrested."

"Don't worry," Elizabeth said. "This will take just a second." She was determined to find out what Bruce's surprise was, and she felt sure that she was on the right track. She also hoped that taking part in the Case of the Four-Legged Creature would help Amy get her mind off her parents.

"This whole thing just seems silly to me," Amy said as they walked toward a small wooden structure that looked like a doghouse.

"Did you hear something?" Elizabeth asked.

"Like what?" Amy asked. "Like a car driving up or something? Should we run?"

"No, it wasn't a car. It sounded like an animal noise!"

"I think you're hearing things," Amy said.

"You've been reading too many mysteries."

"I'm sure I heard something," Elizabeth said as she neared the little wooden box. She peered inside, then jumped back suddenly. "It's a pig!"

"*What's* a pig?" Amy asked.

"In there! There's a pig in there! That's what Bruce is going to let loose in Mrs. Arnette's class on Wednesday," Elizabeth said. She was ecstatic. There were few things that gave her more pleasure than uncovering a mystery, especially if the culprit was Bruce Patman.

"But Elizabeth, you don't even know for sure that's what he was planning," Amy pointed out. "Besides, if you print the story and it comes out on Tuesday, everyone will know the surprise and it won't even happen."

"Exactly," Elizabeth said, beaming. "There's nothing I would rather do than mess up Bruce Patman's chance to cause trouble."

Six

◇

"I talked to Doug last night, and he and Ben talked yesterday, and they want us all to double-date tonight," Janet said to Jessica as they stood in line at the middle school cafeteria.

It was Friday, and Jessica had been anticipating her date with Ben that night from the moment she woke up. "That sounds great," Jessica said enthusiastically as she reached for the last piece of chocolate cake. Before she realized what was happening, the cake was swooped up by somebody else. Jessica spun around to see Veronica with her greedy hands on *her* piece of cake.

"Oh, sorry, did you want this piece of cake?" Veronica asked Jessica with a syrupy-sweet voice and a fake smile. "Here, you can have it. I'm trying not to eat too much sugar anyway."

"And why is that?" Jessica asked as she took the cake from Veronica. "Put on a few too many pounds?"

"*No.* I just want to maintain the weight that I am now," Veronica said in an irritated tone, tucking in her shirt to show off her small waist. "By the way, did I overhear you two saying something about a double date?"

"Yes, you did, as a matter of fact," Jessica boasted.

"Anyone I know?" Veronica asked.

"Probably not, they're both in high school. I'm sure you don't know any high school guys," Jessica said triumphantly, flipping her hair over her shoulder.

"Oh, well, have fun," Veronica muttered and quickly walked away. *There,* Jessica thought with satisfaction. *Serves her right to be jealous.*

"She looked like her dog just got run over by a car when you told her that," Janet said, laughing.

"That will show her not to try to compete with me anymore," Jessica said.

Just then, Aaron and Denny walked up to Janet and Jessica in the lunch line. "Hey, do you two wanna eat lunch with us?" Aaron asked.

Jessica and Janet looked at each other. "Sorry, but we have to sit at the Unicorner today. We have important club business to discuss," Janet said.

"Oh, OK," Aaron said sheepishly. "See you around, then."

"See ya," Jessica said as the boys walked away. She turned to Janet. "It wouldn't have hurt to sit with them for one lunch. Are you afraid that Denny will talk about Tank Fighter again?"

"It's not that exactly," Janet replied. "But remember, we're going out with high school guys now. We can't just go back to hanging out with middle school boys, especially not in front of everyone."

"I guess you're right," Jessica agreed. *After all, what could be better than putting Veronica Brooks in her place?*

"Which do you like better? The Levi's with the purple velvet shirt or the lavender leggings and white oxford?" Jessica was standing in front of the full-length mirror in her bedroom, holding up different outfits. Elizabeth was sitting on Jessica's bed, helping her decide what to wear on her date that night.

"Definitely the Levi's and shirt," Elizabeth said. "That's better for bowling."

"But do you think that it's grown up enough?" Jessica asked, scrunching up her face. "I want him to think I'm mature and sophisticated like a high school girl."

"But you're not a high school girl," Elizabeth

said. "You're only in sixth grade. Just be yourself. This isn't really a date, anyway. You're too young for a real date. You're just going bowling with friends."

"I can call it a date if I want to," Jessica said, tossing her hair.

"Jess, do you really think this is such a good idea?" Elizabeth asked.

"Of course it is. Why wouldn't it be?"

"Well, I just think it's really upsetting Steven. I wonder if it's really worth it to you to get him so mad," Elizabeth said.

"Steven is acting like a total lunatic," Jessica said. "That's his problem, not mine. Do you honestly think I would spend any time thinking about whether Steven is mad at me? I have better things to think about."

"Jess, is there *any* chance you're seeing Ben to bug Steven?" Elizabeth asked. "I mean, would you even be going out with him if it didn't bother Steven so much?"

"How can you even think such a thing, Elizabeth?" Jessica asked. "Ben Oliver is totally cute and mature, and I like him a lot."

"Well, something tells me that you didn't have quite as great a time at Casey's as you said you did," Elizabeth said suspiciously. Elizabeth was an expert at telling when Jessica was stretching the truth.

"As a matter of fact, I did have a great time at Casey's," Jessica said. "Ben is really smart and funny. I wish you'd stop being so down about him. You're starting to bum me out."

"OK, sorry," Elizabeth said. "I just hope you're sure you're interested in him for the right reasons." *And I hope you're ready to handle it when Steven retaliates,* she thought bleakly. *Because when it happens, it's going to be ugly.*

Maybe seeing Cathy will be just what I need tonight, Steven thought on Friday night. He was even a little relaxed, for the first time in what felt like centuries. *I hope the movie's good.*

"'Bye, Mom and Dad," he said, stopping in the living room on his way out. "I'll be back at—"

Suddenly his jaw went slack. His heart plummeted.

There, polluting the furniture with his weasel germs, was Ben Oliver!

"Hi, Steven," Ben said timidly.

Steven glared. *Wasn't it enough that he took away my basketball position and my election, dated my sister, and tried to take away my girlfriend and my best friend?* Steven demanded silently. *Now he has to become buddies with my parents! He does everything he can to ruin my life, and now he acts like we're friends!* It was too much to bear.

"So how are you liking your new job as class

treasurer?" Jessica asked Ben cheerfully, raising her eyebrows at Steven. "Is it as exciting as you thought it would be?"

Steven felt his whole body go tense.

"Actually, it's a lot more hard work and responsibility than I realized," Ben muttered.

"So if you're going to whine and complain about it," Steven asked curtly, "why don't you just let somebody who's up to it do the job?"

"Steven, what in the world is the matter with you?" Mrs. Wakefield asked in surprise. "That's not any way to talk to a guest in this house."

"Well . . . well . . . Are you really going to let Jessica, a sixth grader, go out with someone in high school?" Steven blurted out.

"Mind your own business, Steven," Jessica commanded.

"Jessica's right, young man," Mr. Wakefield said sternly. "It's not really your concern, but since you asked, Ben's father is waiting out in his car to take them to the bowling alley, and I'm going to pick them up."

"Well, I don't think you should let Jessica go," Steven stated authoritatively. "You don't even know him."

Jessica crossed her arms and turned to her parents. "Please tell Steven to stop," she said in a haughty voice. "He's being very rude."

"He certainly is," Mr. Wakefield said crossly.

"Steven, I want you to apologize to Ben and march right up those steps and stay in your room for the rest of the night."

"But I have a date with Cathy," Steven said.

"You heard your father, Steven," Mrs. Wakefield said firmly.

Unbelievable. It is absolutely unbelievable, Steven thought as he walked toward the stairs with as much dignity as possible. It was just too horrible to be true.

This is the last straw, he thought as he stomped up the stairs. *It's time for revenge!*

"Strike!" Ben announced boastfully to Doug as all the bowling pins fell to the ground. "That's my third strike tonight. I'm really on a roll."

"That was great!" Jessica squealed with a big smile at Ben, but he was still staring down the lane at all the pins he'd knocked over.

"I got two strikes myself, don't forget," Doug reminded Ben.

"Your bowling is totally amazing," Janet said. "Two strikes is so awesome."

"Two isn't exactly the same thing as three," Ben quipped.

Jessica and Janet were sitting on the bench behind their lane waiting for their turns to bowl. Jessica was also waiting for Ben to turn around and start paying some attention to her.

How could he be so caught up in a stupid game of bowling when I'm sitting here in my new purple shirt and best jeans? You'd think this was the Olympics or something the way Ben and Doug are acting. But she decided that it didn't really matter. The important thing was that she was out on a real date with a high school guy.

When Jessica got up to take her turn, Ben stood right next to her and took the ball from her.

"Here, try holding the ball like this," Ben advised. "That way, you have more control."

Jessica felt herself tense up. She wasn't an expert bowler or anything, but she'd gone bowling many times before, and she knew what she was doing. Who did Ben think he was to give her pointers? She didn't like criticism from anyone, especially if she didn't ask for it.

"Thanks," she said, sweetly, trying to hide the fact that she was bothered. "That sounds good. I'll try it that way."

Jessica sent the ball down the lane and it veered to the left, landing in the gutter. *Great. Thanks to Ben's stupid advice, and the fact that he's practically standing right on top of me, making me nervous, I roll a gutter ball.*

"You need to take a minute to focus on the pins," Ben said. "You want to aim right for the dead center. It's all about concentration."

"OK. Maybe I'll have better luck this time,"

Jessica said, picking up another ball to take the second try of her turn.

"That's not the right attitude, Jessica. It doesn't have anything to do with luck," Ben instructed.

Who does he think he is—a teacher? One more word and I'll focus on aiming this ball right at him, Jessica thought. Again Ben stood right next to her, and when she leaned over to release the ball, he leaned over, too. The ball started down the center of the lane, then lobbed off to the right and into the gutter.

"Maybe I'll just chuck it with my eyes closed next time," Jessica joked, trying to make light of her disastrous attempt.

Ben looked at Jessica with a frown and scratched his head. "Why would you want to do that?" he asked, looking puzzled.

He doesn't exactly have the greatest sense of humor on earth, Jessica thought.

Jessica sat down as Janet got up to take her turn. Now was the perfect time for Ben to sit down and talk with her, like on a real date.

But Ben stood right where he was in the lane and talked to Doug. "Two weeks ago I bowled one seventy-five," Ben bragged. "And from the looks of the way things are going tonight, I'll probably top that."

"Two months ago I had a one ninety," Doug

said. "I haven't bowled since then, so I'm a little rusty tonight."

"Excuses, excuses," Ben said, shaking his head.

After Janet took her turn, she sat back down next to Jessica. "I only knocked three down," she whispered. "This is pretty embarrassing. They're going to think we're totally spastic."

"We're not spastic, and I don't really care what they think," Jessica said huffily. "I mean, they're acting so babyish about this stupid bowling."

"Shhhh," Janet said. "They'll hear you."

"No, they won't," Jessica said. "They're too busy showing off to each other about their scores."

"I guess you're right," Janet said with a frown, looking over at their dates, who were demonstrating to each other different ways of stepping up to the lane. "And have you noticed how they're barely paying any attention to us except to tell us how to bowl?"

"Notice? How could I not notice?" Jessica asked.

"In fact, they're turning out to be kind of boring. Maybe we should dump them," Janet suggested as she emphatically munched on a pretzel.

"Are you nuts?" Jessica protested. "These are gorgeous high school guys we're dealing with here."

"Hmm. Good point. And it *is* fun to see that irritated look on Lila's face every time their names come up," Janet said.

"My favorite irritated face is Veronica Brooks's," Jessica said, laughing.

Besides, Jessica added to herself, *I can't give Steven the satisfaction of thinking he was right about Ben Oliver. Ben might be boring and annoying, but that's no reason to let Steven have his way.*

"OK, Ben," Jessica said as she walked up to get a ball and take her next turn. She flashed a bright smile at him and tossed her hair back. "Show me again how I should hold it. You *are* the expert, after all."

Seven

◇

"Maybe we'll find something in here," Amy said to Elizabeth on Friday night as they walked into Mr. Sutton's study. Amy's parents had just gone out, and Elizabeth was spending the night, as they had planned.

"I feel a little funny looking through your Dad's stuff," Elizabeth said. "It doesn't seem right."

"I feel weird about it, too, but it might help us understand what's going on," Amy said. "I'm going to go crazy if I don't figure out what's happening with my parents."

"OK. Well, where should we start?" Elizabeth asked.

"Let's look in his desk," Amy suggested as she opened the desk drawer.

"What are we looking for?" Elizabeth whispered.

"I have no idea, but maybe we'll know when we find it," Amy said. "By the way, why are you whispering? There's nobody in the house."

"Oh, you're right," Elizabeth said, raising her voice to a normal pitch. "I guess it just seems that detectives are supposed to whisper. It's supposed to be secretive work." Elizabeth skimmed through the contents of the drawer. "It seems to be mostly bills and papers relating to work stuff."

"Let's look in here." Amy opened a smaller drawer in the back of the desk. She pulled out a stack of mail and looked at the envelopes. Suddenly, her face turned pale and she dropped a letter on the desk.

"What is it?" Elizabeth asked hesitantly as she backed away from the desk. *Don't tell me if it's anything bad*, she pleaded silently. *The whole point of this was to disprove Amy's fears, not to make them worse.*

"See for yourself," Amy said, handing Elizabeth the letter.

Elizabeth held up the envelope and saw that it was addressed to someone named Jane Quigley and it had a stamp on it. "This doesn't mean anything," Elizabeth said, taking a deep breath. *I hope and pray it doesn't mean anything. Just act calm—like nothing's wrong*, she told herself. "It could be somebody he works with or a relative or something."

"Then why is it hidden here in this little drawer and why hasn't he mailed it yet?"

Elizabeth could see that Amy was really getting worked up into a panic.

"Should we try to read it?" Amy asked in a trembling voice.

Elizabeth shook her head. "Look, I'm sure there's a logical explanation. You're just letting your imagination run away with you. Listen, I don't think this is getting us anywhere. Why don't you go make us a snack and I'll clean all this stuff up."

"OK, that's a good idea," Amy said as she played with her hair nervously. "We have some chocolate chip cookie dough. I'll go put some cookies in the oven."

As Amy left the room, Elizabeth put some of the papers and letters back into the desk. She dropped a manila folder accidentally, and when she leaned down to pick up the papers that had fallen out, she froze. There were two pictures of Mr. Sutton with his arm around a woman—and it wasn't Mrs. Sutton! The picture looked sort of old, but still. What did it mean? She turned it over, and gasped when she saw the inscription. "For Rob. Love, Jane," it said. Rob was Amy's dad, and Jane must be the woman he was writing to!

Does this mean that Amy's right? Elizabeth thought with worry. *Maybe something really is going on with another woman.* Elizabeth didn't know what to do. She hated to keep this information from Amy, but she couldn't bear the idea of upsetting her friend. Elizabeth knew there was no way she'd be able to get through an entire evening with Amy knowing what she knew. She slipped the picture back into the folder and put the folder back into the desk drawer.

"Amy," Elizabeth said as soon as Amy came back into the room. "I'm not sure what's wrong with me, but I suddenly have a terrible stomachache."

"Do you think it's that pizza we ate?" Amy asked.

"It probably is the pizza," Elizabeth lied. "Maybe I should just go home and sleep in my own bed. I wouldn't be very good company if I stayed here."

"Well, OK," Amy said. "Thanks a million for coming over here and helping out. I'll call you tomorrow. I hope your stomach feels better."

"Thanks," Elizabeth said on her way out of the room.

"And I just decided to take your advice and not imagine the worst about that letter," Amy said hopefully. "I'm sure you're right about it being a business associate or something."

"I'm sure I am, too. Good night, Amy," Elizabeth said quickly, practically running out of the house. By the time she got outside she really did have a stomachache, but it wasn't from the pizza—it was from imagining how hurt Amy would feel if she found out the truth about her parents.

"Good morning, everyone!" Jessica said to her family as she floated into the kitchen. She was unusually perky for a Saturday morning. Normally, Jessica slept in on the weekends, and when she did finally enter the kitchen, she was still drowsy and grumpy.

"You're in a good mood today," Mrs. Wakefield said as she put a waffle on Jessica's plate. "What's the occasion?"

"I guess it's because I had such a fabulous time on my date with Ben Oliver last night," Jessica gushed.

Elizabeth looked across the table at Steven, who'd dropped his fork on his plate with a loud clanging noise.

"Could you please not say that name? You're going to make me throw up the waffle I just ate," Steven said as he put his hand over his mouth.

"Steven! I'm trying to eat my breakfast! Don't be so gross," Elizabeth said, making a face.

"Oh, I guess you're in a bad mood because you didn't get to go on your date with Cathy last night," Jessica said, pretending to feel sorry for him. "It must be hard for you to hear about other people going out when you had to stay up in your room. Did Mom and Dad even let you watch TV?"

"Jessica," Mrs. Wakefield said in a warning voice.

"You better watch it, Jessica," Steven warned as he squirmed in his seat. "You don't want to see what will happen if you keep bugging me."

"Oh, no, I'm scared," Jessica said, putting her hands to her throat and opening her eyes wide. "What are you going to do? Throw your teddy bears at me?"

Elizabeth was sending Jessica a look that said, *Cut it out. Leave Steven alone.* Unfortunately, Jessica was avoiding her eyes.

"I'm warning you," Steven said.

"Ben is a great guy and he's a super bowler," Jessica said. "I guess he's just a natural athlete. He's so talented at basketball, too."

"Jessica," Mrs. Wakefield said again, her face grim.

"OK, that's it!" Steven exploded. "Now you're asking for it. I know that the only reason you're hanging out with that punk is to get under my skin, and I've had enough!"

"Oh, please, don't flatter yourself," Jessica shot back. "My choice of guys has nothing to do with you, *that's* for sure."

"Stop it, you two!" Mrs. Wakefield demanded.

"Your mother is right," Mr. Wakefield ordered. "Settle down." He shook his head in frustration. "Now, Elizabeth, as a sane person at this breakfast table, can you please explain to your mother and me what's going on."

Elizabeth sighed. "OK, but for the record, I want to say that I'm not taking either side in this battle."

"Thanks a lot!" Jessica said.

"Let your sister talk, Jessica," Mrs. Wakefield said sternly.

"Well, from what I understand," Elizabeth started cautiously, looking first at Jessica, then at Steven, "Ben Oliver won the election for class treasurer, so he's not Steven's favorite person—"

"Talk about understatement!" Steven said hotly.

"Talk about a really stupid reason not to like somebody," Jessica piped in.

"Can you both let Elizabeth finish?" Mrs. Wakefield said wearily.

"Anyway, Jessica likes Ben and wants to hang out with him, and Steven doesn't want her to—"

"As if he has any right to tell me who I can be friends with," Jessica said.

"As if, as my little sister, you have any right to be friends with my enemy," Steven said.

"Enough," Mr. Wakefield said. "Now, here's the way I see it. Jessica's right when she says she can be friends with whomever she wants. But Jessica, you have to stop talking about Ben in front of your brother. We know you're just trying to push his buttons, and you're making everything worse. Now, can we please stop this conversation and eat these wonderful waffles your mother made before they get cold?"

"But Dad, Ben is . . . he's a jerk," Steven protested. "You can't let Jessica be friends with him."

"Mom, he's bossing me around again," Jessica said. "You have to tell him to stop butting into my life."

"Didn't you two hear what your father just said?" Mrs. Wakefield asked. "We're not going to discuss this any further."

Elizabeth let out another heavy sigh. *Poor Amy's family is falling apart, and we're so busy bickering that we can't even appreciate being together.*

I don't care what Mom and Dad say. I'm not going to sit around and let Jessica humiliate me, Steven thought. He was lying on his bed on Saturday afternoon, trying to decide how to get back at Jessica.

The sounds of giggling and screeching voices kept interrupting his thoughts. Jessica was having another one of her Unicorn meetings, and Steven was not in the mood to put up with their noise.

He went out into the hallway, about to burst open Jessica's door to tell them to be quiet, when he heard something that made him pause.

"I wish Veronica would just get over herself," Jessica was saying. "I mean, does she really think she could ever be like me? Could you believe the way she was flirting with Aaron at lunch yesterday? She kept looking over at me to see if I noticed. Ugh! I can't stand her."

Steven stuck his ear against the door to hear better. He was trying his best not to make any noise.

"You guys should have seen the look on Veronica's face when Jessica told her we were going out with two high school guys," Janet said. "It was great."

Everyone in the room started to giggle, and Steven stood back from the door. Giggling girls was one of his least favorite sounds, possibly even worse than fingernails on a blackboard. Besides, he'd heard exactly what he needed to hear. He only needed to figure out where he had heard the name *Veronica* before.

Veronica . . . Veronica . . . Steven thought as he scratched his head. Suddenly it hit him—Veronica was the one who had framed Jessica for stealing her friends' stuff a couple of months ago! This was perfect! Hoping for more details, Steven put his ear back against the door.

"I can't wait till the big junior varsity pep rally and game on Wednesday," Jessica said. "She'll absolutely die when she sees that I'm there as Ben's date."

"You're so lucky," Mary said. "It's such an honor to be there as the date of a high school player."

"Don't forget I'll be there as Doug's date, too," Janet piped in.

"So rub it in our faces," Lila said. "We all have to make an effort to look our best on Wednesday. We want to make a good impression at Sweet Valley High."

"Maybe we should all come over here to get ready before the game," Jessica suggested.

Steven had a huge grin on his face. *You get ready in your way, Jessica, and I'll get ready in mine*, he thought triumphantly. *And thanks to you, I know* exactly *what I'm going to do!*

"I really wish you and Steven would stop fighting," Elizabeth said to Jessica in the family room. It was Saturday night and the twins had rented a movie and popped popcorn. Elizabeth tucked her feet under her as they waited for the movie to start. "I think you shouldn't take each other for granted. Steven's the only brother you have, after all."

"What's with you?" Jessica asked from her

lounging position on the couch. "We always fight. That's what brothers and sisters are supposed to do. Why are you getting so serious all of a sudden?"

"I guess it's because of Amy," Elizabeth said sadly.

"What does Amy have to do with me and Steven?" Jessica asked, putting a handful of popcorn in her mouth.

"If I tell you, you have to promise not to say anything to anyone," Elizabeth said quietly. "Do you promise?"

"I promise," Jessica said. "No offense, but I can't imagine anything happening in Amy's life that would be worth gossiping about to my friends."

"This is serious," Elizabeth said. "It's about her parents. They're having some kind of problems, and Amy doesn't know why. She's afraid they might be getting a divorce."

"That *is* serious," Jessica said, her eyes widening.

"The worst thing is that last night when I was over at her house we found a letter addressed to a woman," Elizabeth said.

"And when Amy left the room, I found pictures of Mr. Sutton with his arm around the same woman," Elizabeth confessed.

Jessica gasped dramatically. "You didn't tell Amy, did you?"

"No, I just couldn't. She's upset enough as it is."

"You're probably right not to tell her," Jessica said. "If Mr. Sutton is involved with another woman, you won't do Amy any favors by telling her. There's nothing she could do about it anyway."

"Do you really think that's what it means?" Elizabeth asked fearfully. She felt a knot in her stomach. She didn't want Jessica to reaffirm her own fears.

"I'm sure that's what it means," Jessica said matter-of-factly. "I've watched enough soap operas to know about these kinds of things."

Elizabeth felt worse than ever. *Amy's whole life is about to fall apart and there's nothing I can do to help her.*

Eight

◇

"What's Steven doing here?" Ellen asked Jessica excitedly. They were standing at Jessica's locker on Monday afternoon, and there was a big commotion coming from down the hall. "You should hear all the girls giggling about how cute your brother is."

"What are you talking about?" Jessica asked as she brushed her hair. "Why would Steven be here?"

"I don't know, but he is," Ellen said.

Jessica looked down the hall and saw the flurry of activity. "Oh, give me a break. You'd think they'd just announced that school was out for the next two months. Don't people have better things to think about than a moron coming to bother his sister?" Jessica asked, rolling her eyes.

"Did you hear about Steven?" Lila asked breathlessly as she and Janet bounded up to Jessica's locker.

"If you mean that for some weird reason he's here—unfortunately, yes," Jessica said. "It's not enough for him to bug me about Ben at breakfast and dinner. Now he has to invade school to give me a hard time here, too."

"Actually, that's not why he's here," Janet said gravely.

"What else would he be doing here?" Jessica asked.

"Should I tell her or should you tell her?" Janet asked Lila with a super-serious tone.

Lila cleared her throat. "I'll tell her," she said, turning to Jessica.

"Tell me what?" Jessica said impatiently. "What's the big mystery?"

"Your brother just asked Veronica to go to the big game on Wednesday as his date," Lila blurted out. "Everyone is totally flipping out, since after all, your brother is considered a total hunk by the entire female population of Sweet Valley Middle School."

Jessica's jaw dropped. "Is this some kind of a joke?" she demanded.

"Unfortunately, it's not," Janet said. "You should see the way Veronica is bragging about it to everyone. You'd think she'd just won an Academy Award or something."

"Why would Steven want to go out with that little witch? How could he date his own sister's worst enemy?" Jessica asked incredulously. "He knows that I can't stand her—" Jessica broke off. Her own words sounded strangely familiar to her.

"What is it?" Ellen asked.

"I know exactly why he's asking her out," Jessica said furiously. "He's trying to get back at me for going out with Ben."

"Well, he did pick a pretty good way to do it," Lila said, barely able to contain a giggle. "Now Veronica Brooks is the biggest envy of the school."

Jessica wanted to sink to the floor out of humiliation. *How dare Steven embarrass me like this! I can just imagine that smug little smile Veronica will have on her face the next time I see her!*

"Here she comes now," Ellen whispered.

Jessica turned around and saw Veronica walking down the hall with a self-satisfied expression. There was a group of girls hovering around her as though she were queen of the school.

"Oh, hi, guys," Veronica said to Jessica and her friends. "Hey, Jessica, maybe Steven and I could double-date with you and Ben sometime."

"I wouldn't count on it," Jessica said, fuming.

"Anyway, I'm sure I'll be seeing more of you now that your brother and I are dating," Veronica said, smiling brightly.

"I wouldn't exactly call going to one basketball game 'dating,'" Jessica said snidely.

Veronica ignored her. "I'll see you around," she said sweetly.

Jessica glared after Veronica, her heart pounding with rage. "She really is the fakest, most obnoxious person I know," Jessica told her friends. "And if she thinks she can outdo me, she has another thing coming!"

"I think that about wraps it up for today," Amy said to Elizabeth in the *Sweet Valley Sixers* office on Monday afternoon. "We've gone over every story at least two times. If we haven't found any mistakes by now, I don't think we're going to."

"Maybe we should go over it just one more time," Elizabeth said. She was trying to steer clear of a conversation about Amy's parents. She was afraid that she wouldn't be able to keep quiet about finding the pictures of Amy's dad if the subject came up. Amy would be hurt as well as humiliated if she found out what Elizabeth had seen. "I just want to make sure that this story about the pig is OK. I can't wait to see Bruce's face tomorrow when he finds out that his plans for bothering Mrs. Arnette's class have been blown out of the water."

"Elizabeth, I'm really tired of reading all that

copy," Amy said. "My eyes are going to fall out if I have to read one more sentence. I have the whole pig story memorized. If I even hear the word *pig* again, I'm going to start screaming and throwing things."

"Speaking of pigs, why don't we go to my house and make some BLTs for an afternoon snack," Elizabeth suggested.

"I don't want a BLT. In fact, after this story, I doubt I'll ever eat bacon again," Amy said. "Look, I really need to talk to you about my parents—"

"I wanted to talk to you about some ideas I have for the next issue," Elizabeth said, quickly cutting Amy off.

"But we just finished *this* issue," Amy groaned. "Can't we talk about the next one tomorrow?"

"No, I need to tell you my ideas before I forget them," Elizabeth said hurriedly.

"Elizabeth," Amy repeated with a serious tone, "I really have to talk to you."

Elizabeth put down the papers she was holding and looked at her friend. She realized that trying to avoid having the dreaded conversation was useless. She couldn't just pretend to ignore Amy when she was feeling so bad. "I'm sorry. Tell me what's up?" she said softly.

"It's just that I've been thinking more and more about that letter. And the more I think about it, the less of a problem I think it is," Amy said hopefully. "I mean, I think you were right when you said it was just a business letter or something. After all, he •works with lots of women. Maybe there isn't anything to worry about after all. Maybe everything is fine between my parents and I've just been imagining things."

"So you're not going to ask your parents if anything is the matter?" Elizabeth asked.

"No, I don't think there's any reason to ask them," Amy said.

Elizabeth took a deep breath. She hated the thought that Amy was happy because she didn't know everything there was to be *un*happy about. And she knew that if the situation were reversed, she'd want to know the truth about *her* parents.

"Amy, there's something I have to tell you," Elizabeth said slowly. "I feel really awful about this, but I found something else in your father's desk when you went into the kitchen the other night."

"What?" Amy asked timidly.

Elizabeth drew in another deep breath. "I found a couple of pictures of your father with his arm around another woman."

Amy's face hardened, and she looked at Elizabeth with a stone-cold expression. "You're a liar!" Amy shrieked. "You just want me to think there's a problem with my parents. You think your family is so perfect! You just don't want me to have a perfect family, too!"

"Amy, how can you say that?" Elizabeth asked desperately. She never felt the least bit competitive with Amy. She only wanted her friend to be happy. She felt as though Amy had just punched her in the stomach.

"I can and *did* say it," Amy said curtly. "I'm getting out of here before you try to convince me of any more lies."

Amy turned around and left the room, slamming the door behind her.

Elizabeth sat alone in the *Sixers* office with a lump in her throat. *I was trying to help and all I've done was make everything worse.*

"Hey, Joe, it's Steven." Steven was on the phone in the upstairs hallway on Monday night, and Jessica could hear him from her bedroom. He seemed to be talking louder than usual.

"I'm totally psyched about Wednesday," Steven said. "Veronica's a total babe. She seems really mature for her age, too."

Total babe? Jessica thought as she squirmed on her bed. *How can he say that gross girl is a babe?*

"Yeah, I know. All the guys on the basketball team were saying they thought Veronica was the cutest girl in the middle school. You'd never even think she was in middle school, since she looks much older than her age."

Jessica was seething. *Veronica Brooks is definitely* not *the best-looking girl in the school!* she thought angrily. She secretly considered herself to be the prettiest girl in school, and she had hoped everyone else thought the same thing. Of course, she and Elizabeth were identical, but Jessica took more care with her appearance, so Elizabeth was only the second-prettiest girl. But *Veronica Brooks*? How could any high school guy even think Veronica Brooks could compete?

"She's totally cool," Steven continued on the phone. His voice even seemed to get louder as the conversation went on. "She'll be my date at the game, and maybe we'll do something else next week. Doug and I were just talking about double-dating with Veronica and your sister. OK, talk to you later. Bye."

Veronica and Steven double-dating with Janet and Doug! Jessica thought in a rage. *Veronica has no right to take my place double-dating with the president of the Unicorns! Steven will pay for this!*

"I just feel sick about Amy," Elizabeth said to Jessica later on Monday night. The two were sitting on Jessica's bed before going to sleep, and Elizabeth had just finished telling Jessica what had happened that afternoon.

"First of all," Jessica said in a solemn voice, "I

think you should have taken my advice and not told Amy." Jessica picked up a hairbrush from her messy floor.

"It's too late," Elizabeth said miserably. "I can't take it back now."

"Look, if Amy were a true friend, she wouldn't have reacted the way she did," Jessica said, flipping her head upside down so she could brush her hair underneath.

"But she *is* a true friend," Elizabeth said. "She's the best friend I have after you. I have to make her understand that I wasn't trying to hurt her."

"I doubt you'll be able to make her understand," Jessica said through the hair that was covering her face.

"Don't say that," Elizabeth cried.

"My advice to you is to let her go," Jessica said authoritatively. "You don't need friends like that anyway. Real friends don't doubt you like that."

"Excuse me? Didn't your friends doubt you when Veronica made them think you were stealing from them?" Elizabeth asked angrily. She didn't usually try to take advantage of Jessica's soft spots, but this time Jessica had it coming to her.

"That was different," Jessica said in a clipped tone.

Elizabeth knew it wasn't different, but she decided to let it go. She was too upset about Amy to argue with Jessica.

"I'm going to go try to get some sleep," Elizabeth said as she stood up and walked toward the door.

"Elizabeth, just forget about Amy and find some new friends," Jessica said. "She's really pretty boring anyway."

Elizabeth sighed heavily and dragged herself out of the room. She didn't care if Jessica thought Amy was boring. Elizabeth loved Amy and hated being in a fight with her.

Nine

"I heard that Oliver won the election by one vote," a voice behind Steven was saying in homeroom on Tuesday morning. "Pretty close, if you ask me."

"Yeah, and I heard the person who cast the deciding vote for Oliver was Cathy Connors," another voice said. "Can you believe that? Wakefield's own girlfriend voted against him."

"That's pretty cold," the first voice said.

Steven felt as though someone had punched him in the stomach. He didn't even bother to turn around to see who was talking. It would be too humiliating if they realized that he'd overheard them. Everything suddenly became clear to him.

Cathy voted for Ben because she has a crush on

him, Steven thought as he slid down in his chair. He felt as if he wanted to disappear. *How could she betray me like that? She was my campaign manager. She pretended to be on my side the whole time, then she turns around and votes for Ben.*

Now Steven was even more fired up for his date with Veronica. He would get his revenge on his sister *and* on his double-crossing girlfriend at the same time!

"Wait, Jessica," Elizabeth said as they were heading down the hallway on their way to social studies class Tuesday morning. "There's Bruce and he has a copy of the *Sixers*."

"I'm surprised he can even read," Jessica joked.

Elizabeth watched as Bruce threw the paper on the floor. He looked up and spotted her. Elizabeth quickly turned and started in the opposite direction. "Hurry," Elizabeth said to Jessica. "He's coming toward us."

"Stop right there, Elizabeth Wakefield!" Bruce shouted. "Don't think you can get away so easily."

"Hi, Bruce," Jessica said, smiling brightly. "How sweet of you to be so excited to see my sister today." She turned to Elizabeth. "Come on, Elizabeth, we'll be late for Mrs. Arnette's class. I hear she's having a special farm-animal demonstration today."

"You'd better stop now, Elizabeth, or I'll follow you around all day!" Bruce threatened.

"Ooh, scary," Jessica said.

"What's new, Bruce?" Elizabeth asked brightly.

"What's new?" Bruce repeated angrily. "I'll tell you what's new. You've been snooping around where you don't belong."

"Whatever are you talking about?" Jessica asked innocently. "Sister, dear, do you have any idea what he's talking about?"

"No, I can't imagine," Elizabeth said, stifling a giggle. "Let's go to class. I just love farm animals."

"Don't think you're getting away with this," Bruce said as Jessica and Elizabeth walked away.

"I already did," Elizabeth shouted back. *And it serves him right, too. I can't wait to tell*—Elizabeth's happiness quickly faded as she realized she couldn't share the plan's success with Amy. It seemed wrong that she couldn't. After all, the two of them had broken the story together.

Elizabeth walked into class and took a seat way in the back. She knew she shouldn't sit in her regular seat next to Amy and upset her any more than she already had.

"I'm so excited about our double date," Veronica was saying to Janet at the Unicorner on Tuesday.

"What double date?" Jessica asked as she

slammed down her tray, causing her milk carton to fall over. *What is Veronica doing at the Unicorner?* Jessica wondered.

"Steven and I are going to Casey's next week with Doug and Janet," Veronica gushed.

"Is that true, Janet?" Jessica asked, clenching her jaw.

"Actually, it *is* true," Janet said sheepishly. "Doug called me last night and asked me if I'd go with him and Steven and Veronica, and I really wanted to see him again, so I said yes. Doug said it was Steven's idea."

I just bet it was Steven's idea, Jessica thought, fuming.

"How could you?" Jessica asked Janet.

"We can talk about this later," Janet said.

"I really feel great about the fact that I'll be spending more time with the Unicorns," Veronica cooed. "Between dating Jessica's brother and double-dating with Janet, I'll be almost a Unicorn by association."

"I seem to recall that you already tried to be a Unicorn and it didn't exactly work out," Jessica said nastily. "Now, could you please leave our table. This is the Unicorner, which means it's for Unicorns, which means you don't belong here."

Veronica stood up, smiling brightly. "I'm sure I'll be seeing you guys later. We all have so much to gossip about together now."

Jessica turned to Janet with an angry glare. "How could you let her sit here after everything she did to us? You know I can't stand her. What happened to Unicorn solidarity?"

Her friends gave one another a look that Jessica knew well. It was the way the Unicorns looked at each other in the presence of a non-Unicorn, a person who wasn't in on their secret.

"What's going on around here?" Jessica asked, totally offended.

"Maybe we should give Veronica another chance," Lila said. "I mean, people *do* change, and she is dating someone in high school, after all. That makes her very good Unicorn material."

"But she's a fake! She framed me for robbery and she stole from every one of you," Jessica exclaimed. "You can't just forget something like that!"

"Well, you *could* see her stealing as a demonstration of just how badly she wants to be a Unicorn," Ellen said.

"I can't believe you guys," Jessica said as she stood up to leave.

"That seat is taken," Steven growled at Cathy on Tuesday in the Sweet Valley High lunchroom. She was starting to sit down at the table that the two of them always sat at together.

"What do you mean, it's taken?" Cathy asked. She looked completely bewildered, and Steven wished she didn't have to look so pretty.

"I don't eat with traitors," Steven said. "Why don't you go sit with Ben Oliver. I'm sure he'd like the company."

"What are you talking about?" Cathy asked. "What's wrong with you?"

"What's wrong with me? I'll tell you what's wrong with me. I have just a little problem with the fact that you *acted* like my girlfriend and *pretended* to be my campaign manager and then you turned around and voted for Ben Oliver, who you think is so incredibly cute!" Steven said, pratically shaking with fury.

"B-but I—I . . . Let me explain—" Cathy stammered.

"Aha! So it's true!" Steven exclaimed.

Cathy's face was stricken. "It's true, but there's a good explanation. Howie Farber and I—"

"I don't want to hear it," Steven said as he stood up. "I don't want to hear whatever stupid excuse you're going to try to make up."

She actually admitted that she voted for him, Steven thought in disgust as he stormed away. He knocked his chair to the floor. *My own girlfriend is in love with my enemy!*

"Hi, Elizabeth, can I talk to you?" Amy said to Elizabeth as she approached her locker on Wednesday morning.

Elizabeth felt a little tremor of nerves. She was afraid that Amy was just going to get mad at her all over again. She wasn't up for another awful scene like the one the day before. It was just too painful.

"I'm really sorry about what happened yesterday," Elizabeth said, avoiding Amy's eyes. "It was wrong for me to get involved in your family's business. I should have just stayed out of it. But I do want you to know that I never meant to hurt you."

"I know that," Amy said. "I'm the one who's sorry."

"What are you sorry for?" Elizabeth asked.

"I said some pretty rotten things to you yesterday," Amy said.

"I understand why you said them," Elizabeth said.

"You were trying to help me and I see that now," Amy admitted. "I just got so upset by what you told me, and I didn't want to accept that it could be true. I wanted so badly to think that you were lying. Unfortunately, I know now that you weren't."

"How do you know?"

"I looked in my father's desk last night after my parents had gone to sleep," Amy confessed. "I saw the pictures you told me about."

Elizabeth looked at her friend sympathetically.

"Maybe we shouldn't assume the worst," she said, trying to sound hopeful. "Maybe they're pictures of a cousin you've never seen or heard of before. She could be a family friend or something."

"Thanks for trying to make me feel better, but I might as well face it. I'm sure the woman in the picture is the same woman he wrote that letter to—and that's no cousin," Amy said, her voice shaking. "I hope you'll forgive me and still be my friend even though I said those awful things yesterday."

Elizabeth gave Amy a hug. "Of course I'm still your friend, and I'll always be here for you."

"I have a feeling I'm going to need a friend now more than ever," Amy said as she and Elizabeth walked down the hall to their first class.

"Where's my brush?" Jessica asked frantically. She and the other members of the Unicorn Club were in her bedroom on Wednesday afternoon getting ready for the big game. The room was a total disaster area.

"OK, I need everyone's attention," Janet announced as she stood in front of Jessica's full-length mirror. "Do I wear my hair up or down?"

"Definitely wear it up," Mary advised. "That makes you seem older."

"But I was going to wear my hair up," Jessica

said. "We can't wear our hair the same way."

"Of course you can," Lila told her. "Stop being so babyish."

Jessica shot an angry glance at Lila. *If I'm so babyish, how come I'm the one going out with a high school guy and not you?* Jessica thought as she shook her hair out of the braid she'd been making.

"Jessica, do you think I could borrow something of yours?" Mary asked. "I don't think this shirt is right for the game."

"You're right about *that*," Lila said. "That collar is so dumb-looking—not exactly the image we want for the Unicorns. What's with that ruffle, anyway?"

"Sorry," Mary said defensively. "My mother gave it to me for my birthday. I wasn't thinking when I wore it to school today."

"You can borrow anything you want," Jessica said. "Only you don't have to worry, that shirt isn't dumb. It's nice. I don't know who made Lila the authority on how we're supposed to look." *Mary's shirt is pretty juvenile, but I'm not going to give Lila the satisfaction of agreeing with her*, she thought.

"Thanks, Jessica. You're the greatest," Mary said as she sorted through the items in Jessica's overflowing closet.

"Jessica, do you think Ben and Doug will give us jerseys with their numbers on them to wear?"

Janet asked excitedly. "That would be the coolest thing of all."

"I bet they will," Jessica said.

"I doubt it," Lila said. "It's not exactly like you're their girlfriends yet."

"Well, we'll just see when we get there," Jessica said.

"We better get moving or we'll miss the beginning of the pep rally," Ellen said.

"Remember to pay attention to the cheerleaders at the rally," Lila told everyone on their way out of Jessica's room. "We might get some helpful ideas for our own cheers."

Jessica took one last look at herself in the mirror. *I definitely look older than a sixth grader,* she thought, checking her blue jeans, white T-shirt, and black vest. *I could pass for a freshman any day. Sweet Valley High—here I come!*

Ten

"I don't think they're so much better than we are," Janet said as the Unicorns watched the junior varsity cheerleaders during the basketball game. "So far, I haven't seen them do one move that isn't in the Boosters' routine."

"No way, Janet," Lila argued. "Some of their gymnastics are pretty awesome. Did you see the back flip that girl just did?"

"That *was* pretty incredible," Tamara agreed. "She made it look so effortless."

"Hey, does anyone have lip gloss?" Ellen asked.

"Here," Tamara said as she handed Ellen her lip gloss. "Who has breath spray?"

"I do," Lila said. "Hey, Ellen, can I have that lip gloss after you?"

"Does anyone know what the score is?" Jessica asked.

All the Unicorns looked at one another, then broke into hysterical giggles. "I guess we're not exactly here for the game," Mandy said.

"Speak for yourself," Jessica said as she focused her eyes on the game for practically the first time. "I happen to like basketball."

"Yeah, right," Lila said, rolling her eyes.

"I'm bummed that Doug and Ben didn't give us their jerseys to wear," Janet said to Jessica. "That would have been so cool."

"Ben told me his extra jersey was in the laundry," Jessica lied. "I'm sure Doug's is, too."

"It looks like someone on the team gave Veronica a jersey," Mary said. She pointed to where Veronica was sitting on a bleacher down in front.

"Number sixty-seven," Ellen said. "Whose number is that?"

"That's Steven's number!" Jessica shrieked. "I can't believe it! How dare he do that to me!"

"Steven gave his jersey to Veronica. I don't really see where you fit in," Lila pointed out. "It's not like he did anything to you, Jessica."

"Oh, yes he did," Jessica insisted. "The only reason he gave Veronica his jersey was to get back at me for seeing Ben."

"Well, Veronica's certainly getting a lot of attention because of that jersey," Tamara said. "Look at all those freshman girls she's sitting with."

"Yeah, it looks like she's made a bunch of new high school friends," Ellen added.

Jessica looked down at Veronica, who was laughing and talking loudly. She noticed that Veronica kept turning around to make sure Jessica saw her. Jessica was seething.

"Ben just made a basket," Janet said to Jessica.

Jessica jumped up from her seat and shouted *"Go, Ben!"* at the top of her lungs. She saw Steven dart an evil eye at her from the court. *Take that, Steven Wakefield*, she thought as she sat back down.

"Steven just scored, too," Mary said excitedly.

"Way to go, Steven!" Veronica was shouting even louder than Jessica had.

"She's making me sick to my stomach the way she's acting like she's my brother's girlfriend," Jessica said. "Did you see what a big deal she made about him scoring?"

"It's not as if you're Ben's girlfriend any more than Veronica is Steven's, and you just did the same thing she did," Lila said.

"That's completely different," Jessica said crossly.

"Oh, really? How?" Lila asked, raising one eyebrow.

"It just is, that's all," Jessica said.

"Maybe we should ask her to sit with us," Janet suggested. "She seems to be really popular with the freshmen."

"If you ask her to sit here, then I'm leaving," Jessica said, her cheeks flushed with rage. "She *is* my worst enemy, as you very well know. She's just acting like her usual phony self with those girls. I'm sure they'll see through her act in a few minutes."

"Just because one Unicorn doesn't like someone, doesn't mean the rest of us can't be friends with them," Lila said in an irritatingly sweet voice. "We do want to be in with the people at Sweet Valley High, after all."

How can my friends be so fooled by her? Jessica thought. She sat silently with her arms folded in front of her and fumed for the rest of the game.

"Great game," Janet said as everyone got up from their seats. "They really killed Big Mesa. Jess, we should be proud of our brothers. They were definitely the stars of the game."

Great, that's really what I want to hear, Jessica thought. Her already foul mood was becoming worse. "I think Ben was the star. In fact, I'm going to go tell him that."

Jessica stepped over the bleachers and went down to the court. She ran up to Ben, who was standing next to Steven, and threw her arms around him. "Ben! You were fantastic! You were by far the best player on the court today. You're the reason Sweet Valley won."

Ben looked embarrassed, awkward, and confused. "Gee, thanks, Jessica," he said, disentangling himself from her embrace. "But it wasn't all just me."

"You're so modest," Jessica gushed loudly.

"Steven!" a voice behind Jessica shouted. "You were sensational!" Jessica whirled around and saw Veronica throwing herself at Steven.

"Everyone said you were the star of the game," Veronica shouted. "I'm so proud to be wearing your jersey."

"You look so pretty today, Veronica," Steven said with a glance at Jessica. "Why don't you come with me for a postgame celebration with some of the freshman class."

"I'd love to," Veronica practically sang out.

"So, Ben," Jessica said, "are you going to any postgame parties?"

"I can't," Ben said. "I have too much to do. Now that I'm class treasurer I barely have time for anything else."

"Oh, OK, then, I'll see you later," Jessica said forlornly as Ben walked into the locker room. *How humiliating and unfair that Veronica gets to go to a high school party and not me!*

Just as she thought her mood couldn't get any worse, she saw the Unicorns—her best friends—swarming around Veronica in admiration.

"Hey, Veronica," Lila chirped. "I hope you'll call me tonight when you get home and tell me all about the party."

"Oh, of course I will," Veronica said. "I'll remember every itty-bitty detail."

"You're so lucky," Ellen gushed. "I would give anything to go to a party like that."

That girl is lucky I'm not a violent person, Jessica thought as she walked out of the gym alone. *If I were, I'd stuff her in that basketball hoop!*

"What's all the commotion about?" Elizabeth asked Jessica as the two girls walked into school on Thursday morning.

"I don't know," Jessica said, looking toward the end of the hall, where people were buzzing excitedly. "Maybe school was canceled for the day. That would be nice for me, considering I didn't do any of my homework last night."

"Why didn't you do it?"

"I was too upset after that stupid game yesterday," Jessica said, still looking toward the end of the hall. "I couldn't concentrate on anything. I kept seeing Veronica's fake smile as she accepted Steven's invitation to go to that party."

"Just put that girl out of your mind," Elizabeth

said. "We both know she's just a show-off. Don't let her get to you like that. Come on, let's go see what's going on."

Elizabeth and Jessica walked to the end of the hall and saw a swarm of girls and guys around Veronica's locker. Most of the crowd was made up of Unicorns.

"So was there dancing?" Lila asked Veronica.

"There was a little dancing," Veronica said nonchalantly. "But mainly people were just sitting around having mature conversations."

Jessica was fuming. Veronica was obviously bragging about the party she'd gone to with Steven and she was milking it for everything she could. *Don't let that stupid, fake Unicorn-wannabe get to you*, Jessica kept trying to tell herself. *She doesn't even deserve your attention.*

"That sounds really cool," Tamara said.

"It was," Veronica said snottily. "It reminded me of my old school. We used to have a lot of get-togethers like that. I'm so relieved to finally find a social life like I was used to."

Here we go with that "social life" business again! Jessica thought, remembering that that was one of the things that had first irritated her about Veronica—when she first got to Sweet Valley she was always putting down their school and saying how much better her old school was. *I wish you'd never left your stupid school!* Jessica wanted to shout.

"So who was at the party?" Ellen asked.

"Everyone on the basketball team except for Ben Oliver. And all the cheerleaders were there," Veronica chirped.

"What were the cheerleaders like?" Lila asked.

"They were really cool," Veronica said. "They were all super nice to me. In fact, the captain of the cheerleaders invited me over to her house tomorrow."

"Wow, that's great," Janet said. "I wish Doug had invited me to the party."

"You would have loved it," Veronica said. "Oh, hi, Jessica. You would have loved the party, too. I'm sorry Ben didn't go. We could have all hung out together."

Jessica let out a loud laugh. "You're joking, right? I can't think of anything less fun than sitting around with a bunch of sweaty basketball players while they talk about the play-by-play of the game," Jessica lied. "It sounds like a major boring party. You couldn't have paid me a million dollars to go to a party like that."

All the Unicorns looked at Jessica as if she'd just announced she was moving to Tibet.

"Well, whatever," Veronica said. She headed to class as the crowd followed, hanging on her every word.

"Can you believe she's acting like a celebrity just because she went to one party?" Jessica asked Elizabeth as everyone walked away.

"No, I can't," Elizabeth agreed. "She really is the most obnoxious person in this school. But remember what I told you."

"I know, I know," Jessica said. "I'm trying my hardest not to let her bug me. But how much can a person take?"

Eleven

"What do you think of this blouse?" Jessica asked Elizabeth, holding up a pink-and-white striped silk blouse. The twins were shopping in the Valley Mall on Saturday afternoon.

"Don't you think that's a little grown-up-looking for you?" Elizabeth asked, making a face. "It looks a little stuffy. Not really your style at all."

"Now that I'm seeing a high school guy," Jessica said, flipping her hair, "I have to start dressing more sophisticated."

Elizabeth shrugged. "I don't think you should change the way you dress because of some guy," she said.

"I'm sure Todd wouldn't care if you wore pigtails and overalls, but that's because he's just a kid."

"Even if Todd did tell me to wear certain kinds of clothes, I wouldn't unless they were things I felt comfortable in," Elizabeth said.

"Look, everything's different with older guys," Jessica said authoritatively.

"Hey, look. There's Lila," Elizabeth said, looking across the mall.

"It couldn't be," Jessica said. "She said she was staying home today because she wasn't feeling well." Jessica was flipping through a rack of clothes and didn't even bother to look up.

"I'm sure that's Lila," Elizabeth said. "She's with Janet and somebody else. I can't tell who it is. I can only see the back of her head."

Why would Janet and Lila come to the mall without calling me first? Jessica wondered. Shopping in the mall together on Saturdays was a Unicorn tradition. Jessica looked out into the mall and saw that the third person with Janet and Lila was Veronica!

"What are they doing with *her*?" Jessica gasped.

"I don't know, but they're heading into this store," Elizabeth said.

"Quick! Come here," Jessica said. She grabbed Elizabeth's hand and pulled her down on the floor underneath a rack of clothes.

"Can you please tell me what we're doing down here?" Elizabeth whispered as a belt buckle hit her on the head.

"Shhh," Jessica urged. "We're spying. Don't make a peep. Don't even breathe."

"The things I put up—" Elizabeth started to say before Jessica slapped her hand over Elizabeth's mouth.

"They're here," Jessica whispered urgently.

"This is the cutest store," Veronica said cheerfully. "I'd love to find something here to wear on my date with Steven on Monday when we go to Casey's."

"It's really cool that you're going out with him again," Lila said. "He's considered the best-looking freshman guy at Sweet Valley High. That's a real score for you."

Jessica was smoldering with rage as she heard them moving clothes around on the racks.

"It really would be neat if you and Doug and Steven and I started doing things together," Veronica said.

"And Jessica and Ben could join us," Janet said. "Then we could all six do things together."

"I doubt that would happen," Veronica said. "Jessica really doesn't like me. No matter how hard I try to be her friend, she just snubs me. I've apologized a million times for that little incident that happened earlier this year, but she won't forgive me."

You fake, lying witch! Jessica almost yelled out.

"Maybe Doug and Steven could set me up

with one of their friends and the six of *us* could do stuff," Lila said.

"That's a great idea," Janet said. "I'll ask Doug if he knows anyone who would be good for you."

"Tell him to make sure he's cute," Lila said, setting off a round of giggles.

"I found the perfect shirt," Veronica announced.

"That would look great on you," Lila agreed. "It's very sophisticated."

Jessica heard the sound of the cash register and the voices of Janet, Lila, and Veronica trail off as the door of the store opened and closed. She pulled Elizabeth up and they both took big breaths.

"I thought I was going to pass out down there," Elizabeth said. "There wasn't any air under all those clothes. Especially since you were trying to suffocate me!"

"Can you believe Veronica?" Jessica asked. "She's totally brainwashing my friends. She's trying to steal them away from me again."

"She really is icky," Elizabeth agreed. "But your friends will realize what she's up to. Don't worry. She tried that once before and it didn't work."

Unfortunately, it almost did work, Jessica thought sullenly, remembering how close she had come to losing her friends because of

Veronica. She couldn't let that happen again.

"Can we go outside now?" Elizabeth asked, waving her hand in front of her sister's face. "I really need some air."

"Sure. I just want to buy that blouse first." Jessica looked through the rack where she'd seen the white-and-pink silk blouse, but it was gone.

"Excuse me," she said to the saleswoman at the counter. "There was a white-and-pink striped blouse over there that I wanted to buy, but I can't seem to find it now."

"One of those young girls just bought it," the woman said.

"Hi, Steven," Cathy said to Steven on Monday morning. She was sitting at her usual desk in biology class, right next to Steven. "Do you think we could talk for a minute?"

"We have absolutely nothing to talk about," Steven told her.

"Hey, Cathy, thanks for last night," Howie Farber said on his way to his seat.

What's going on here? Don't tell me Cathy's seeing Howie and Ben! Isn't it enough that she's seeing my archenemy? Does she have to see my archenemy's friend, too? Steven thought to himself. "So is Farber one of your new boyfriends, too? Do you alternate days—you know, see Oliver one day and Farber the next?"

"You're really being ridiculous," Cathy said. "I've been tutoring Howie in math. That's one of the things I wanted to talk to you about."

"Yeah, right," Steven said sarcastically as he stood up. "I guess you figure I'm pretty stupid. You can save your lame explanation, because I already know what you're going to say."

"But Steven. Wait! Can't we go to Casey's this afternoon and talk calmly about this?" Cathy pleaded. "I know you'll understand if you'll just give me a chance."

"I already have a date this afternoon," Steven said. "In fact I'm seeing Veronica Brooks, who's considered by many people to be one of the best-looking girls in all of Sweet Valley." Steven stood up and walked to the other side of the room to sit in another seat.

"Hey, man, how are you liking being class treasurer?" Steven overheard Doug asking Ben in the locker room after basketball practice on Monday afternoon. Steven was on the other side of their lockers sitting on a bench, so they couldn't see him listening to their conversation.

"It's pretty lousy, to tell you the truth," Ben answered him. "I almost wish I'd never been elected at all."

"It can't be that bad," Doug said.

"Oh, yes it can," Ben said. "I'm so preoccupied

about it that I totally messed up today in practice. I'm sure the coach won't want me to keep playing center after today."

"Don't sweat it," Doug reassured him. "We all have off days. So what's so bad about being class treasurer?"

Steven heard Ben take a deep breath. He couldn't imagine what could be so bad either. *Probably Ben's just such a wimp that he's not up to the job,* Steven thought as he leaned closer to the lockers to hear better.

"Basically, Howie Farber really messed things up when he was class treasurer, and now our class is missing two hundred and eighty dollars," Ben said.

"How did he manage to do that?" Doug asked.

"He's not good with numbers and he didn't keep track of the budget," Ben said. "Now I have the job of trying to raise two hundred and eighty dollars. The worst part is that I have to raise it by next month, because that's when we're supposed to go on our class trip to Disneyland."

"Wow, what a bummer," Doug said sympathetically. "That's going to be a lot of bake sales and car washes."

"Tell me about it," Ben said wearily.

"Did a lot of the class already know about it when the elections were held?" Doug asked. "Do you think people voted for you as some kind of bad joke?"

"No, the only person who knew about it until today besides Howie was Cathy Connors."

"And how do you know that she knew?"

"Because she called me last night to see if I would explain the situation to her boyfriend, Steven. Apparently, she cast the deciding vote for me because she wanted to protect Steven from being stuck with the big debt. Howie told her about it, since she's been tutoring him in math. Now Steven thinks there's something going on between Cathy and me."

Steven put his head in his hands. *How could I have been such a fool?* he asked himself. *How could I have doubted Cathy like that?*

Steven felt terrible. Cathy was only trying to protect him. She found out about it because she'd been tutoring Howie in math. That's what she'd been trying to explain. *I'll have to find her right away and tell her that I understand everything!*

"Are you going to tell Steven?" Doug asked.

"I'm almost afraid to," Ben said. "Ever since I got his position on the team and especially after this dumb election, I think he really hates me. That's too bad, too, since he seems like a pretty cool guy."

Ben thinks I'm a cool guy, Steven thought. *Unbelievable. Maybe I should forget about my stupid date with Veronica*. He thought about it for a minute, then decided he had to go through with the date. *I don't want to give that annoying sister of mine the satisfaction.*

When Steven heard Ben and Doug get up to go, he quickly and quietly squeezed himself into a locker until they walked past. Once they were gone, Steven bounded out of the locker room, determined to go on his date with Veronica and get his revenge on Jessica.

Steven stopped by a florist on his way to meet Veronica that afternoon. The flowers weren't for his date, however—they were for Cathy. Before he could pick up Veronica, he had to try to make peace with Cathy.

With the bouquet of daisies in his hand, he ran to Cathy's house and up the front steps. His heart was pounding from running and from nerves as Cathy opened the door.

"What are you doing here?" Cathy asked. She looked both surprised and angry. "If you're here to yell at me some more, I really don't want to hear it."

"These are for you," Steven said breathlessly as he handed her the bouquet.

For a minute, Cathy looked as if she was about to smile. Instead, she handed back the daisies and started to close the door. "You really hurt me, Steven. You just assumed the worst about me without giving me the chance to explain everything to you."

"I know, and I'm really, really sorry. I understand now why you voted for Ben—"

"It doesn't really matter anymore," Cathy said, cutting Steven off. "I have to be somewhere." Cathy slammed the door and left Steven standing on the porch.

He leaned down and gently placed the flowers on the ground in front of the door, then walked off slowly and sadly to Veronica's house.

Twelve

"I couldn't believe it when I saw Veronica sitting at the Unicorner again today. The worst part was that not one of my friends came over to me when they saw me sitting at another table," Jessica said to Elizabeth on Monday afternoon as she tried on her tenth outfit. She was getting dressed for her date with Ben that afternoon. He was going to pick her up and take her to Casey's. He'd suggested that they go somewhere else, since they'd already gone to Casey's on their first date, but Jessica wasn't going to miss seeing Steven with Veronica for anything.

"It *is* strange that they were willing to forgive Veronica for everything she did to you and the Unicorns."

"I know," Jessica said, pulling on a purple

minidress. "And the worst part is, the only reason they're being nice to her is because of *our* brother."

"Steven did think of a pretty smart way to get back at you," Elizabeth said, sitting back on Jessica's bed.

"Thanks a lot, Lizzie," Jessica pouted. "I can't even talk to my friends about how awful Veronica is anymore. They think she's wonderful," Jessica complained as she pulled her hair back in a French twist. Normally, she wore her hair down, but she wanted to look more grown up for her date.

"Well, you know you have *my* support. I haven't forgotten how awful Veronica was to us," Elizabeth consoled.

"That's the doorbell!" Jessica shrieked. "Is my hair OK? Do you like my dress?"

"You look gorgeous," Elizabeth said. "Have fun. I'll see you in a few minutes. Amy and Maria are stopping by and we're going to Casey's ourselves. I wouldn't miss this for anything."

"That's such a beautiful shirt you're wearing, Steven," Veronica cooed in a syrupy-sweet voice. "It really brings out the color of your eyes."

"It's just a T-shirt," Steven said.

Steven and Veronica were sitting at a booth in

Casey's with Janet and Doug. Steven thought the afternoon would never end. He couldn't leave until Jessica and Ben got there, but he didn't think he could endure Veronica a minute longer. She'd already complimented him five times. It was getting embarrassing. And when she wasn't flattering him, she was going on about how great *she* was.

"Did I tell you that my family is going to Europe this summer?" Veronica asked, fluttering her eyelashes.

"Wow. That sounds great," Steven said. "You're really lucky."

"Actually, I've already been there three times. I'm almost starting to get sick of it. You can't imagine what a bore it is to go into every single old church in Europe." Veronica giggled loudly, and Steven's neck stiffened. She had one of the loudest, most irritating giggles he'd ever heard.

"So maybe you should give your ticket to somebody who would appreciate the trip," Steven said sarcastically.

"I don't get it," Veronica said, giggling. "Why would I give my ticket to someone else?"

"Never mind," Steven said under his breath.

"I really like your sister Jessica," Veronica went on in a sickeningly sweet voice. "Unfortunately, she doesn't really seem to like me."

And I can see why, Steven thought to himself.

He looked up from his hot-fudge sundae for practically the first time since he'd sat down and saw Cathy walk into the restaurant with Howie Farber.

That's it. Now I've really done it! Cathy's with Howie! Steven thought wretchedly.

"I think I have a good chance of becoming a Unicorn," Veronica said. "In fact, the only thing keeping me from being one is your sister."

Steven watched Cathy and Howie at the front of the restaurant. They were smiling, their heads bent close as they talked across the table. Even though Steven knew Cathy wasn't really interested in Howie, he couldn't help feeling jealous. Especially since they were having such a good time while he had to sit there listening to Veronica rattle on about the dumb Unicorn Club.

"Why would you want to be a Unicorn in the first place?" Steven asked.

"Shhhhh," Veronica said, pointing to Janet, who was apparently too involved in her conversation with Doug to care what they were saying. "Because they're the most popular girls in school. I'm just as popular as they are, so I really should be one. Maybe you could talk to Jessica for me."

"Sure thing," Steven said dismissively. He was too preoccupied watching Cathy and Howie to really listen to Veronica.

Steven was getting ready to walk over to

Cathy's table just as Jessica walked in with Ben. Jessica was obviously trying to call attention to herself by laughing loudly as she walked through the restaurant. She sat down at a booth right across the aisle from where Steven was sitting.

Steven looked back at Veronica to see if she'd noticed their entrance. Not only had she noticed, her gaze was glued on Jessica and Ben.

"Are you friends with him?" Veronica asked, still staring at them.

"Who? Ben Oliver?"

"Yeah. I thought you might be friends, since you're on the basketball team together and he's seeing your sister," Veronica said.

Steven laughed to himself. "No, we're not friends exactly," he said. "Why?"

"He just seems like a cool guy," Veronica said, smiling in Ben's direction. "And he's pretty cute."

What is it with this guy? Steven thought in annoyance. *Why does everyone think he's so cute?* The more Veronica stared at Ben, the angrier Steven felt.

"We went to that fancy restaurant, La Maison Jacques, last night," Maria Slater said to Elizabeth and Amy after they'd settled into a front booth in Casey's that afternoon. "We all had lobster and my parents had champagne."

"What was the occasion?" Elizabeth asked as she glanced toward the back of the restaurant. She was trying to observe Steven and Jessica on their dates. From what she could tell, everything was going pretty smoothly. "Was it somebody's birthday?"

"No, it was my parents' seventeenth wedding anniversary," Maria said as she took a big bite of her banana split.

"That sounds really nice," Amy said quietly.

Elizabeth noticed that Amy had that sad look she'd had so often lately.

"Actually, it was pretty annoying," Maria said, rolling her eyes.

"Why was it annoying?" Amy asked.

"My parents were so lovey-dovey with each other that it became almost nauseating," Maria said. "They kept talking about the first time they met, and they described their first five dates down to practically every last detail."

"I think that sounds really sweet," Amy said wistfully.

Elizabeth wished that Maria would stop talking about how happy her parents were. She knew that it was making Amy feel worse than she already did.

"The worst part was the way they kept holding hands and kissing each other," Maria said, scrunching up her face. "It was gross. I could barely eat my dinner."

"I think you should be grateful that your parents are still so much in love," Amy said. "You should realize how lucky you are."

Elizabeth was trying to keep her attention on her friends, but she couldn't help glancing back in Steven and Jessica's direction. Their voices kept getting louder and louder.

"Sometimes I almost wish they weren't so in love," Maria said.

"How can you say that?" Elizabeth asked, refocusing on her friends. "That's horrible."

Maria sighed. "I know. I don't really mean it like that. But they're so into each other it's almost as if I'm not there," she complained. "Like, sometimes when we're all at the breakfast or dinner table I'll have some story to tell them, and they'll be so busy making goo-goo eyes at each other that they barely pay any attention to me."

"I think that's a terrible attitude," Amy said vehemently. "Maybe you should imagine what your life would be like if your parents weren't so in love. What if they weren't even living together? What if they got a divorce?"

Maria looked completely stunned. "But that would never happen."

"You never know," Amy said. "It can happen to anyone's family. It could even happen to yours!"

"That's such a mean thing to say," Maria cried. "What's wrong with you today?"

"Look!" Elizabeth said loudly, trying to put a stop to their conversation. "What's going on back there?"

"That cracks me up!" Steven said with a big booming laugh. *I can play the same game you're playing, little sister*, he thought.

"What cracks you up? What did I say that's so funny?" Veronica asked as she finally redirected her attention to Steven.

"Oh, nothing," Steven said with another loud laugh. "I was just remembering a funny joke."

"What's the joke?" Doug asked, talking to Steven for practically the first time that afternoon.

"It's funnier if I keep it to myself," Steven lied. "Hey, Veronica, did I tell you how pretty you look today?" he asked loudly, sneaking a glance at Jessica.

"Thanks, Steven," Veronica said, blushing.

"In fact, I think you're one of the prettiest girls at Sweet Valley Middle School," Steven boomed.

"I've heard you're the best basketball player at Sweet Valley High," Jessica practically shouted at Ben. "A couple of people told me you're the best center the school ever had."

Steven noticed that Ben's face was turning a

weird shade of red and he seemed to be muttering something.

"I think you'd be a great Unicorn, Veronica," Steven yelled. "The best. And you'd be an amazing Booster, too. From what I've seen, they could really use some help."

Ha! Steven thought triumphantly, when he felt something fly across his right cheek. Something red and gooey. He looked down in amazement and saw a cherry in his lap. He knew instantly who had thrown it. He peered at Jessica, who looked completely absorbed in her cherry-less sundae.

He plucked the cherry from his own sundae and threw it across the aisle. It smacked Jessica right in the nose. *Yes!* Steven thought proudly. *Pretty good shot, if I say so myself.*

"Steven, why are you throwing food at your sister?" Veronica asked with a giggle.

"Did I throw something?" Steven asked innocently. "It must have flown off my spoon accidentally."

Just then, a big ball of whipped cream flew past Steven and landed on Doug's head.

"Hey, what's going on?" Doug demanded, putting his hand to his gooey hair. "Where did that come from?"

"I think Jessica threw it," Veronica whispered, her eyes wide.

Doug was so angry, his face turned pink. He glared at Jessica. He stood up, picked the mushy banana from his banana split, and fired it at her. Jessica shrieked as it smeared all over the front of her purple dress.

By now everyone in the restaurant was watching them in amazement.

"OK, that does it!" Jessica shouted. She rushed across the aisle with her sundae and dumped the whole thing on Steven's head.

Everyone in the room gasped.

"Jessica! Doug threw the banana, not me!" Steven shouted, wiping off the ice cream that was dribbling down his face.

"Oh, yeah?" Jessica demanded, glaring at Doug. "Then this is for you!" Jessica took the remains of Janet's strawberry milk shake and sloshed it into his lap. Pink goo splattered all over Janet's suede jacket, too.

Janet shrieked, and before Jessica could apologize, Janet picked up the remains of Doug's banana split and hurled it at Jessica. Jessica dodged it and the sundae went flying over her shoulder . . . and pelted Lila Fowler.

Steven watched as the entire restaurant erupted in chaos.

Ice cream was flying and people were shouting.

"Ahhaaagh!" he heard Veronica scream as a frothy chocolate milk shake splashed the front of her pink and white blouse. Steven couldn't help smiling.

Suddenly he spotted Howie Farber. This was the perfect opportunity to get back at Howie. Steven aimed a spoonful of ice cream at his head. It flew through the air, but Howie ducked at the critical moment. The glob landed on Cathy's cheek and oozed down her face.

For a second Cathy looked stunned.

Steven held his breath. He'd really done it this time, he thought dejectedly. Cathy would never forgive him after this.

Then, to his incredible happiness and relief, Cathy started laughing. She picked up a bowl of lime Jell-O from a nearby table and hurled a wobbly green handful at Steven.

"STOP IT!" a loud and angry voice shouted over the noise.

The restaurant immediately grew quiet. With a sinking heart, Steven looked up and saw Mr. Casey himself, standing at the back of the room, looking as if he were about to explode.

"Did you see that bulging vein in Casey's forehead?" Steven asked the group of ice-cream-covered students standing in front of the restaurant.

Minutes before, Mr. Casey had yelled and screamed and thrown every single one of them out of the shop.

"I know," Jessica said. She'd been laughing so hard, she could barely catch her breath. "I thought he was going to have a heart attack."

"I don't think I'll ever eat ice cream again," Elizabeth said, wiping a blob of ice cream from the front of her T-shirt.

"You won't need to," Amy added. "You can just eat your clothes."

Elizabeth was glad to see Amy laughing along with the rest of them. It was the first time in days that she'd seen her friend having fun.

"So where'd your date go?" Jessica asked Steven.

"I think we scared her off," Steven said. His stomach hurt, he'd been laughing so hard. He looked at Jessica, whose hair was sticky with ice cream, and smiled. "She probably won't want anything to do with our insane family ever again."

"Good!" Elizabeth, Jessica, and Cathy shouted in unison.

Suddenly Jessica was laughing again. She was laughing so hard, no sound was coming out. She pointed across the parking lot.

Steven watched in amazement as two people walked off together hand in hand.

It was unmistakable. It was incredible. It was totally perfect: Ben and Veronica.

Thirteen

"So, where's the lovely Miss Veronica Brooks today?" Jessica asked her friends as she sat down at the Unicorner on Tuesday at lunch. "I thought she was your new best friend."

"After yesterday, I think she changed her mind about wanting to hang out with us," Janet said, laughing.

"And now she's got a new high school boyfriend," Mandy added.

"I'm sure neither of *you* will ever go out with a high school guy ever again," Lila said to Jessica and Janet, flipping her hair over her shoulder. "Ben and Doug weren't exactly impressed by your behavior."

"Sure they were impressed," Jessica said, trying to suppress a smile. "I look so great with milk shake on my head."

"What are you so happy about, Jessica?" Ellen asked. "I thought you liked Ben. Now he's going out with Veronica, your worst enemy."

"Oh, please," Jessica said. "She can have him. I have better things to do than listen to some guy blab on and on about what a great bowler he is."

"Yeah, really," Janet piped in. "Doug's just as boring. He and Ben and Veronica were in a big huff about the food fight yesterday. How exciting is that?"

"Maybe they're just a little *too* mature," Jessica said.

"I can't believe what I'm hearing," Tamara said. "I mean, how could you dump high school guys?"

"There are more important things than dating high school guys, Tamara," Janet informed her.

"Yeah," Jessica agreed, biting into her hamburger. "For instance, dating totally cool middle school guys." She threw a glance at the next table over to where Aaron was eating potato chips and looking especially cute in his L.A. Dodgers cap.

"Like Denny," Janet said.

"Like Aaron," Jessica added with a sigh.

"I'm so relieved that the whole class-treasurer mess is behind us now," Cathy said to Steven. They were sitting at Casey's with Jessica and Elizabeth, celebrating the end of the Ben Oliver–Veronica Brooks war.

"You and me both," Steven agreed as he plunged his spoon into his hot-fudge sundae. "I have to admit it would stink to be in Ben's shoes right now. Spending money sure beats raising it, I always say."

"How can you eat that sundae after yesterday?" Elizabeth asked. "Didn't you have enough ice cream to last you for the rest of the year?"

"I never got to eat mine yesterday," Steven said. "None of it ever landed in my mouth."

Jessica gave a small gasp. "Guess who just walked into Casey's together?" she asked.

Everyone turned around to see Ben and Veronica walking in. Veronica sat down at a booth as Ben walked over to their table.

"Hi, Ben," Steven said cheerfully. "Want to sit with us?"

Ben looked a little surprised, but smiled anyway. "No, thanks. I'm here with Veronica. I just wanted to tell you that now that I'm so busy trying to figure out a way to get back the class money, I'm going to have to drop the basketball team."

"Wow," Steven said. "Bummer."

"Yeah, it is," Ben agreed. "Anyway, I talked to the coach after practice, and he said you can play center again—that is, if you still want to."

"Of course I want to," Steven said. "And good luck with being class treasurer."

"Thanks," Ben said, shaking his head. "I'll need it." He walked back to Veronica, who gave him a huge smile, then looked right at Jessica and tossed her hair.

"Look at her gloat over being with Ben," Elizabeth said to Jessica. "Aren't you peeved?"

"No way," Jessica said, licking whipped cream off her spoon. "That boring guy can eat ice cream with any stupid, annoying girl he wants, for all I care."

"I just hope he likes girls with incredibly irritating giggles," Steven added. "Veronica's laugh makes me think of fingernails on a blackboard."

Steven and Jessica were laughing when a shadow fell over their table.

"Uh-oh," Jessica whispered.

It was Mr. Casey. And he still looked mad. "What are you troublemaking Wakefields doing in my restaurant?" he yelled. "I told you I never wanted to see your faces again."

Steven winced. Elizabeth's face turned pale. "W-we're really, really sorry about yesterday," Elizabeth stammered.

"Is there anything we can do to make it up to you?" Steven asked politely.

"Yes, there is," Mr. Casey huffed. "You can leave. Now!"

Steven, Cathy, Jessica, and Elizabeth stood up to leave. "Geez, that makes two days in a row that I haven't been able to eat my sundae!" Steven muttered on his way out the door.

"This casserole is delicious," Elizabeth said to Mrs. Sutton. It was Tuesday night and Amy had invited Elizabeth over for dinner. Amy said it was too depressing when it was just her and her parents.

"Thanks," Mrs. Sutton said simply.

"So," Elizabeth began, trying to fill the uncomfortable silence, "I'd love to learn how to make it. What's in it?"

"Tuna, noodles, peas, cheese, and pepper," Mrs. Sutton said distractedly, looking down at her plate. A long silence followed.

"Um . . . what kind of cheese?" Elizabeth pressed.

"I don't know. Whatever was in the fridge."

Elizabeth fidgeted with her napkin as another uncomfortable silence filled the dining room. "Amy and I have been really busy working on the *Sixers*," she said. "Amy's doing this great article on school lunches."

"Thanks," Amy offered weakly.

Elizabeth poured herself some more water from the glass pitcher, even though she wasn't really thirsty. *I'd suffocate in this house if I had to spend every night like this*, she thought. *No wonder Amy's been so miserable.*

Elizabeth looked at Mr. Sutton, who hadn't uttered a single word since he sat down. "So how's work, Mr. Sutton?" Elizabeth asked politely.

Mr. Sutton looked as though he just realized that he was sitting at a table with other people.

"Fine," he said tightly.

I'm getting nowhere fast, Elizabeth thought unhappily. She was relieved when the phone rang and broke the silence.

"I'll get it," Amy said quietly as she stood up from the table and walked into the kitchen.

What a change from my house, Elizabeth thought sadly. Whenever the phone rang at the Wakefields', everyone stampeded to answer it first.

Amy walked back into the dining room. Her face was as white as the tablecloth. "Dad," she said, her voice trembling. "It's for you. Someone named Jane."

Elizabeth drew in a sharp breath. "Jane" was the name on the letter she'd found in Mr. Sutton's desk drawer.

Mr. and Mrs. Sutton exchanged somber glances before Mr. Sutton left the room. Amy looked at Elizabeth with eyes full of worry.

After just a few moments, Mr. Sutton came back to the dining room. "Amy, honey, your mom and I need to have a private talk with you."

He turned to Elizabeth apologetically. "I'm sorry, Elizabeth. Do you mind heading home a little early tonight?"

"N-no. Not at all," Elizabeth said numbly and got up from the table.

Amy walked Elizabeth to the front door with tears running down her cheeks. "This is it," Amy whispered. "The days when we were a happy family are gone for good."

What will happen to Amy's family? Find out in Sweet Valley Twins and Friends #83, **Amy's Secret Sister.**

SIGN UP FOR THE
SWEET VALLEY HIGH®
FAN CLUB!

Hey, girls! Get all the gossip on Sweet
Valley High's® most popular teenagers
when you join our fantastic Fan Club!
As a member, you'll get all of this really
cool stuff:

- Membership Card with your own
  personal Fan Club ID number
- A Sweet Valley High® Secret
  Treasure Box
- Sweet Valley High® Stationery
- Official Fan Club Pencil (for secret
  note writing!)
- Three Bookmarks
- A "Members Only" Door Hanger
- Two Skeins of J. & P. Coats® Embroidery
  Floss with flower barrette instruction
  leaflet
- Two editions of *The Oracle* newsletter
- Plus exclusive Sweet Valley High®
  product offers, special savings,
  contests, and much more!

Be the first to find out what Jessica & Elizabeth Wakefield are up to by joining the
Sweet Valley High® Fan Club for the one-year membership fee of only $6.25 each
for U.S. residents, $8.25 for Canadian residents (U.S. currency). Includes shipping
& handling.

Send a check or money order (do not send cash) made payable to "Sweet Valley
High® Fan Club" along with this form to:

SWEET VALLEY HIGH® FAN CLUB, BOX 3919-B, SCHAUMBURG, IL 60168-3919

NAME _____
_____(Please print clearly)_____

ADDRESS _____

CITY_____ STATE _____ ZIP_____
_____(Required)_____

AGE _____ BIRTHDAY_____ /_____ /_____

Offer good while supplies last. Allow 6-8 weeks after check clearance for delivery. Addresses without ZIP
codes cannot be honored. Offer good in USA & Canada only. Void where prohibited by law.
©1993 by Francine Pascal   LCI-1383-123